This Young Girl Passing

UNBEARABLE BOOKS / AUTONOMEDIA

SERIES EDITORS: Jim Feast and Ron Kolm

THIS YOUNG GIRL PASSING

DONALD BRECKENRIDGE

Typeset and cover design by Walter Chiu.
Illustration by Tom Motley.

First American Paperback Edition
ISBN: 978-1-57027-234-9
Unbearable Books are published and distributed by
Autonomedia
POB 568 Williamsburgh Station
Brooklyn, NY 11211-0568 USA
info@autonomedia.org
www.autonomedia.org
www.unbearables.com

NYSCA
New York State Council on the Arts

This publication is made possible
in part with funds from the New
York State Council on the Arts,
a state agency.

Acknowledgments

With gratitude to Johannah Rodgers, Stefanie Sobelle, Jennifer Zoble, Walter Chiu, Tom Motley, Theodore Hamm, Jim Feast and Ron Kolm.

"Sunday, August 7, 1977" appeared in *Fiction International*; "Monday, April 19, 1976" and "Friday, March 28, 1997" appeared in *Numéro Cinq*; Friday, October 22, 1976 appeared in *The Brooklyn Rail*; "Sunday, July 4, 1976" appeared in *Salt Hill*; "Monday, April 19, 1976" and "Friday, March 28, 1997, Part II" appeared in *The Unbearables Big Book of Sex* (Unbearable Books/Autonomedia, NY, 2011).

for Johannah Rodgers

"This young girl passing by eternally
with her hands in her pockets,
or so it seemed: what has become
of her since she crossed the street more
than twenty years ago?"

Eugene Ionesco
from *Present Past Past Present*
translated from the French by Helen R. Lane

Sunday, August 7, 1977

"I mean," Robert said, "I'll wake
up in the middle of the night and you're like the only thing I think
about," while holding the joint between the index and middle
fingers of his right hand, "even now." A thin cloud appeared in
front of his face, "After all this time has gone by," and dissipated
as he passed the joint to Sarah, "that's funny in a way." She nodded
and tried to change the subject, "What are your parents fighting
about?" "Money…the bank loans, hospital bills." Robert was sitting
cross-legged on a flat gray rock. A seed popped as the orange ember
at the end of the joint grew thicker. Sarah was sitting on a tree
trunk. He watched her take another drag. Broad bands of sunlight
were filtered through the trees surrounding them. She was wearing
cut-off jeans and a frayed army fatigue jacket unbuttoned to her
navel. A thin stream of smoke was carried along by the breeze.
The sleeves of her jacket were rolled up to her elbows and hid a
large bruise on her left arm. "I was thinking about converting the
garage into an apartment," Robert picked at the pimple on his

chin, "that way I wouldn't have to hear their bullshit anymore." Her bare feet were resting in a clump of velvety moss, and her leather sandals were next to the blue cotton blanket they'd just had sex on. Sarah slowly exhaled and passed the joint back. "You know, carpet the floors, install a wood-burning stove and buy one of those little refrigerators," he carefully tapped the ash onto the right knee of his jeans, "I might even get a new stereo," looked up and noted her bemused smile, "it would be like my own apart-ment." She shook her head, "You'd be better off just moving out and renting a place up in Utica." He rubbed the gray ashes into his faded blue jeans, "I can't afford that right now," with the tip of his index finger, "but maybe then we could spend the night together." She wiggled her toes in the moss while saying, "I like it here." He was grateful she had finally agreed to see him again, "Well, it's a lot better than the backseat of my dad's car," and after telling him she was on the pill, "I mean that was pretty intense," insisted he not use the condom in his wallet. She thought of his father's Ford Falcon, "I always liked getting high with you," with its wide dark blue backseat. Robert realized that the condom had been in his wallet for so long that it was probably useless, "yeah," and silently vowed not to let her hurt him again, "we had some fun together." Sarah cleared her throat, "When I saw your dad at the store the other day he looked like his grouchy old self to me." A ladybug landed on his T-shirt. "Yeah," he muttered, "I guess," and placed the joint between his lips. She pointed at his heart, "You've got a guest." "The bank is probably going to foreclose on the store," he looked down and exhaled, "it just doesn't seem to faze him." "Come on," she coughed into her clenched fist, "that store is his entire life." "I think the stroke he had," Robert passed the joint back, "took out a big part of his brain," then picked the ladybug off his shirt, "we've got these," and put it on the palm of his right hand, "frozen burritos now," after it climbed to the tip of his middle finger, "that you microwave," the spotted shell opened, "they taste just like dog food," and its wings appeared, "not that I would know what dog food tastes like," before slowly flying away. A crow cawed from above the trees. She exhaled, "You've really changed since you graduated last year," Robert glanced at her warily as she added, "I haven't gotten high all summer," while passing him the joint, "isn't that bizarre?" The droning cicadas grew louder as a cloud moved before the sun. Robert had been so excited about seeing her, "I just feel like I've been shit on…" that he hadn't fallen asleep until three in the morning, "that's all." The joint was cold between his fingers. She rolled her eyes, "Here we go again." He placed it on the rock, "Haven't you heard anything I've been saying?" She nodded, "All I've heard come out of your mouth is this fucking, tidal wave of self-pity. Poor you. Poor you, and your fucked-up life. You tell me I'm not listening to you, and you, you haven't heard a single word I've been saying." Robert had been listening, "That isn't true," but Sarah hadn't said anything he wanted to hear, "I just think things are totally screwed up with me right now and it isn't going to change, because people don't change. I mean," he swallowed hard, "you're born a certain way and that's it," before snapping his fingers, "I'll be like this till I die and maybe if I'm lucky I won't have to wait that long." "Just listen to yourself," she began to mope, "I'm gonna turn my parents' garage into an apartment and buy a new stereo and then I'm gonna get really stoned." He laughed, "That isn't funny, Sarah." "What happened to your father is terrible…it really is. And yes your family sounds incredibly fucked up," he nodded, and she quickly continued, "we've all got problems, Robert," before he could interrupt, "and if you could think about anyone other than yourself for more than five seconds you'd probably stop feeling so sorry for yourself." She did care about him, otherwise, why would she be saying this? "I've really missed you," he leaned forward, "just hanging out and kicking the shit around," while looking closely at her blue eyes, "all my other friends are gone or they're brain dead." She leaned toward him, "You just had a bad year." He nodded, "That's putting it mildly." "Well, why don't you put it behind you." He sighed wistfully, "I had everything going for me when we were together." Sarah looked away before asking, "What about college?" He frowned, "With what money?" "Didn't your dad's insurance cover the cost of the hospital bills?" He cleared his throat, "Not even half of it," and spit on the ground. A bird landed on the branch of a nearby tree and began to sing. Robert slowly counted to ten in his head before asking, "Why are you on the pill?" Sarah had graduated in June and spent all of July locked in her bedroom, "Because it's my body and," the summer was going by so fast, "I want to be on the pill…" she had filled three spiral notebooks with poems and stories of unrequited love, "if that's alright with you." A breeze forced the birch trees to bend and sway. She recalled the weatherman's warning of a chance of thunderstorms in the afternoon, but it hadn't looked like rain when they parked his dad's car by the side of the road. He thought about them speeding west on a Greyhound bus, "Don't you want to go to California with me?" She closed her eyes, "You could get a scholarship," and shook her head slowly from side to side. "We could leave tonight." "You had a B average and that's good enough." He would empty the safe in the back of the store, "It was a solid C minus," and maybe if they made it look like a robbery, "besides we look like money on paper," then disappeared without a trace they could get away with it. "That's just bullshit and you know it." They could live in a small bungalow by the ocean under aliases, "Close enough," although he knew she would never agree to it, "besides it wouldn't make that much of a difference." "Why not?" What he needed was a willing accomplice, "You've got to want to do something before you go and do it. Otherwise..." shrugging his shoulders emphatically, "what's the point?" "Talking to you right now is just like talking to a fucking wall." He grinned, "You know I'm turning eighteen next month," before singing, "it's only just begun." "So how are you going to get out of here then," she pursed her lips, "on a spaceship?" "Yeah," he slowly unfolded his legs, "just like Luke Skywalker," and placed his feet on the ground before standing up, "I was seriously thinking about joining the Marines." "You're kidding," she blinked twice, "right?" He bit his lower lip to keep from laughing, "Your brother has been telling me about it and it doesn't sound a hell of a lot worse than standing behind a counter all day micro—" "My brother," she glared at him, "was lucky to come home alive and there aren't that many—" "It's nineteen seventy-seven," he gave her a mock salute before sitting down, "at least they would pay for college." Thunder rumbled faintly in the distance. Sarah wasn't sure if he was serious, "There aren't a lot of opportunities in America for crippled vets." The forest grew darker. "I like your brother, you know, you should call him more often." She felt a chill in the air, "I always knew you were a real man." Robert grinned, "He grows *real* good weed." The marijuana her brother grew by Schuyler Lake was potent, inexpensive, and it had been available all summer long. She said, "My point exactly," while buttoning up her jacket. "So Sarah, what's with all this charity?" "What charity, what are you talking about?" "Don't you think you owe me an explanation?" "I apologized." He crossed his arms beneath his chest, "There is a big difference between an explanation and an apology." "You haven't heard a word I've said since we had sex," her eyes narrowed, "I guess you don't need to listen to me now that you've gotten what you wanted."

5

He coughed into his clenched fist, "I've been waiting for my explanation." "What happened was that," she looked down at her toes, "I was going to move to New York City with my boyfriend right after graduation," and sighed, "he was supposed to leave his wife for me." "His wife?" "But he got cold feet," she didn't look up, "and just dropped me—" "His *wife*." Sarah ignored him, "or he was just lying the entire time." "Who is this guy?" Robert sounded incredulous. Her hair blew into her face, "I need you to listen to me now…okay?" The air smelled of rain. "I knew you dumped me for someone else. I just couldn't figure out who it was and Laura wouldn't tell me." She frowned, "I'm not friends with her anymore." Infrequent drops began falling on the leaves. "Since when?" "Since I discovered she couldn't keep her big fat mouth shut," Sarah began to wonder if telling Robert was a mistake, "can you?" He nodded, "Sure." "Promise me that this will not get past you," she looked closely at his bloodshot eyes, "because it could hurt a lot of people." A raindrop hit the back of his neck, "Who am I going to tell?" and he looked up at the dark sky. "You've got to promise." Exhaling through his nose, "Girls can be so melodramatic sometimes." "I'm not," she crossed her arms beneath her breasts, "I'm very serious about this." He placed his palms on the rock, "You have my word," and leaned back, "now, who was it?" She closed her eyes, "Bill," and listened to the rain falling, "Bill Richardson." Furrowing his brow, "Who is that?" Damp splotches darkened the rock around his hands. "You know who that is." "Who," a loud thunderclap rolled above them, "the French teacher?" She nodded, "That's him." "Holy shit," Robert hadn't taken French but he knew Mr. Richardson, "you're kidding right?" She watched him in silence, "So that's why," as he tried to respond, "I mean, you were going to go live in New York City with him?" "Don't you think we should be getting back to the car?" He stood up slowly, "We can talk about it there," while looking at her in disbelief. She walked over to the blanket, "I can't let this get wet," and balled it up in her arms.

Thin streaks of rainwater ran down the drying windshield. Robert said, "I think you did this because you want people to think you're crazy." The humid air smelled of their wet clothes. "No, I did it because," Sarah's long fingers were caught up in her damp hair as she brushed it out, "nobody can find out about this." He placed his left hand on the knob and rolled the window all the way down. The Queen Anne's lace lining the road swayed in the breeze and shed the large drops of water that had collected in its umbels of white flowers. She watched the gray clouds move across the sky. Thin rivulets of water were slowly running down the dark blue hood. "Well," his right arm was draped over the back of the seat, "I think you told me because you're trying to be so extreme." "Bullshit." "You're like, 'I can trust him with this because I know it'll freak him out and then he'll have to forgive me for dumping him,'" he turned to her, "and I think that's really petty and, and calculating of you." The blue cotton blanket was spread out on the backseat. "Come on," she shook her head, "we didn't go out for that long." Crickets in the nearby ditch began to chirp. "How long were you with him for?" She looked at the radio on the dashboard and wished it worked. Sunlight broke through the clouds and illuminated the open meadow on the opposite side of the road. "You're making it seem like it's my fault that you're lonely." Large clumps of flowering milkweed dotted the meadow. "It is." A hawk followed an uneven circle on the ground as it spiraled through the sky. "Who is being calculating now?" He sighed, "You were the only person I wanted to be with." She leaned back in the seat, "You can't blame me for that," clasped her hands, "and it isn't my

7

fault that I was in love with someone else," and let her voice trail off, "that he broke my heart." He removed his arm from the back of the seat, "How long were you with him for?" She slid over to her window, "a long time." He watched as she rolled the window down. A monarch was pushed along by the breeze. "How long is that?" She watched it struggle to settle on the leafy branch of a swaying bush. "You took two years of French." She was slow to respond, "I took three years of French." "Jesus Christ," he winced, "since you were fourteen?" "It got serious when I was a junior...that spring," turning to him, "if you know what I mean." He looked at her closely and then shook his head. She pushed her bangs away from her eyes while he stared at her. Sarah looked out the window and waited for him to speak. A car appeared in the distance. "Sixteen...that's statutory rape." It was moving toward them with its headlights on. "And how old is he?" The faint sound of tires on wet pavement. "Bill just turned thirty-two." Robert looked down at her long legs, "Bill," and thought about how much he'd missed her, "will be lucky if someone doesn't chop off his nuts." "It was worth it," Sarah turned to him, "and maybe one day you'll be lucky enough to love someone the way I did." He placed his hands, "So you were seeing him," on the steering wheel, "while we were going out?" She nodded, "Yeah well," and watched the headlights of the oncoming car, "you were more like a summer thing." The key was already in the ignition. He muttered, "Thanks," under his breath, "thanks a lot," and realized she was serious. He just had to turn the key while pressing his foot on the gas pedal and the car would start. The dark green Plymouth speeding toward them looked very familiar. He wanted to drive her home and then go off somewhere by himself and get really baked. She sank back into the seat, "Oh shit." "What," Robert placed the thumb and forefinger of his right hand on the key, "that's not your dad is it?"

8

She shook her head, "That's his wife's car," and crouched lower. He turned the key in the ignition, "You are crazy," and stepped on the gas. The Fury swept past them and he got a good look at the woman driving it. He recognized her from the store, "So that's his wife," and recalled that she always paid with a check. Sarah quickly turned around, "She's alone," and watched the car speed away. The engine revved beneath the hood. "Can we go to Dairy Queen now?" she asked. He shifted the car into drive, "No," and pulled onto the road. "Come on, you can buy me a sundae." "Blow me." She laughed, "Only if you buy me a sundae." He stepped on the gas, "No way." She slid across the seat, "Please," and put her left hand on his thigh as the car picked up speed.

Sunday, February 23, 1997

Bill pulled the heavy wooden door open for Sarah. "You know," she turned to him after walking into the dimly lit bar, "I've never been in here before." The door closed behind them, "Really," as he stood beside her, "would you like to go somewhere else?" The warm air was permeated by the smell of stale cigarettes and spilt beer. She shook her head, "Have you?" The bartender looked up from his paperback and nodded. The long discolored mirror reflected the length of the empty bar. "Oh…" Bill considered her question, "once or twice." The fluorescent light suspended above the pool table illuminated its felt surface. They stepped forward, "I've passed it a million times but I've never been inside," she glanced at their reflection in the mirror and added, "isn't that strange?" "When you think about how long it's been here," he conceded with a nod to their reflection, "then again," before turning to her, "there's always a first for everything."

When she swayed into his side, the honeyed scent of her perfume caused him to smile, "Is this okay?" The hands of the Budweiser clock mounted on the wall above the mirror indicated that it was fifteen past two. "This is just perfect," she unbuttoned her black overcoat, "Where should we sit?" He pulled off his leather gloves, removed the navy blue balmoral from his head, "Wherever you'd like," and brushed the snow off of it. She noticed that his hair was gray, "I really don't care." With a nod to the booth overlooking the window facing the street, "Over there?" A green neon shamrock was quietly buzzing in the center of the window. "Okay," she remained by his side, "why don't we sit over there." The muted afternoon light brightened the varnished oak tabletop. The bartender stole another glance while turning the page. Bill scanned the liquor bottles lining the shelves, "What would you like to drink?" She looked at the Guinness and Budweiser handles on the beer taps, "A coffee if they have it...no wait," and clutched his forearm, "I think I'll have a glass of wine instead." Bill frowned. She removed her hand, "What's the matter?" "The Irish aren't known for their wine." She shrugged, "I really wouldn't know the difference." "Very well," he chuckled, "red or white then?" "White...no red," furrowing her brow, "red wine," before quickly asking, "unless you think I should get something else?" He wanted to embrace her again, "I think you should get what you want." She nodded, "Red wine," then looked at him expectantly, "what are you going to have?" "A pint of stout...I suppose." She tugged at his forearm, "Hmmm," and imitated the sound of his voice, "the Irish aren't known for their stout," while shaking her head. "Is that so?" She winked, "You get it and I'll sit down before someone takes the table," then walked across the worn tile floor. She removed her coat and draped it over the back of the red vinyl seat.

Sarah's memory of the first day they'd kissed no longer felt like a story that might have happened to someone else. The day he said, *You know I really care about you and I always want you to tell me the truth*. She recalled the warmth of his smile—the shape of his lips—just before they kissed, and removed the compact from her purse.

Bill stepped up to the bar and placed his hands on the back of a stool. The bartender looked up, "What can I get for you two?" "I'll have a pint of Guinness," Bill cleared his throat, "and she would like a glass of red wine." "Okay," he lay the paperback on the bar, "the Guinness is going to take a minute so why don't you sit down and I'll bring it to you." Bill nodded, "What's that you're reading?" "Cervantes," the bartender put his right hand on the bar, "his novellas." Bill noticed the unplugged CD jukebox in the mirror, "This must be a good job for reading." "It is on Sunday," the bartender offered, "Would you like me to turn on the radio?" Bill shook his head, "Not if it's going to disturb your reading," then crossed to the booth, "he'll bring the drinks over," removed his jacket, then draped it over her coat before sliding into the seat across from her, "the stout takes time."

She closed the silver compact and put it back in her purse. The bartender tuned in a Sibelius overture. Bill rested his palms on the oak tabletop and noticed her dark red lipstick. The bartender unscrewed the cap on a jug of Burgundy and carefully poured the wine into a water glass. The pipes began knocking as the radiator by the door began to hiss.

Sarah turned away from the window and asked, "So what brings you to downtown Utica on this pleasant afternoon?" Bill drummed his fingers on the table, "that's a very good question," then explained, "I was on my way back from Riverside Mall, and I thought I'd go through town instead of taking the highway back," he looked around the bar, "I was even thinking about having a drink on my way home." She looked skeptical, "What were you doing at Riverside Mall?" "I was just returning something for Mary," he confessed, "it's a great way to get out of the house."

Bill had been driving up Genesee to the intersection at Elizabeth when the light turned red. Sarah's heels resounded along the sidewalk as she approached the camera store. A bread truck raced through the intersection as he noticed a tall blonde in a black overcoat enter the camera store on the opposite side of the street. The Asian woman behind the counter informed Sarah that the pictures hadn't come in yet and repeated her promise to call as soon as they did. The light changed from red to green and the driver of the white Cadillac behind Bill lay on his horn. He recognized her as soon as she pushed open the door and stepped onto the sidewalk. She watched a battered white Cadillac with a blaring horn speed through the intersection. Snow began falling as the black Volkswagen Jetta came to a stop across the street. She was standing on the opposite side of the street with her hands in her pockets and a broad smile on her face. Bill almost ran across the street, and then they embraced. Sarah placed her head on his shoulder while telling him how happy she was to see him again. He asked her where she was going, and did she have any time to talk, and maybe they could get a drink or something.

Sarah leaned back in the seat, "That was my next question." "I was," he laughed nervously, "I was just going to ask you about that," noting the thin gold wedding band on her left hand, "you're married now." "Fifteen years this July, and we have a daughter. Her name is Kate. She wants to be an actress? Can you imagine that?" "Fifteen years..." Bill kneaded his chin, "I can't believe that," as he took her in, "that this is finally happening to me...you know," then exclaimed, "you know you look fantastic!" The bartender cleared his throat while approaching the table, "Here we go." They thanked him in unison as he placed the drinks down, "Would you like to start a tab?" Bill leaned back in the booth, "That would be just fine." The bartender nodded, "Alright," and walked away. Bill clutched the pint in his right hand, "Well, cheers." Sarah raised her glass, "Cheers," sipped the wine, and grimaced. He laughed, "Is it that bad?" "I'll get used to it," she placed the glass on the table, "Steven and I had some really nice wines in France...even the cheap ones were really good." Bill rested his left arm along the back of the seat, "Steven is your husband?" "Yes," she nodded, "we just got back from Paris," and placed her palms on the table, "he took me there for Valentine's Day." He studied her fingers before asking, "How long were you there for?" She glanced out the window, "A week," as a bearded black man pushing a shopping cart filled with car batteries rattled by. "Was that your first time?" She turned away from the window and nodded, "I can't wait until we go back." He regarded the stout settling in the glass, "How is your French?" Sarah squirmed in her seat, "I was afraid you were going to ask me that." He looked at her expectantly, "How did you do?" and when she didn't respond he persisted, "Did you remember any of it?" "A bit," with a blush, "we got some Berlitz cassettes in January and that helped, *a lot*," Bill nodded wittingly as she continued, "I was really pretty surprised by how much I actually remembered, and when you make an effort most French people really respect that and," she picked up her glass, "most of the time their English was much better than my French," and sipped her wine. "That's very true," placing his elbows on the table, "you know that's what I tell my students." "I remember you saying that," she ran a hand through her curly blond hair, "everyone was a lot nicer than we thought they would be," then looked out at the falling snow, "it's kind of funny running into you like this." The snow had left a faint cover on the parked cars. "Why?" Sparse traffic moved quietly along the avenue. "I've been thinking of you a lot lately…" "Really?" "I mean…because I was speaking French," she turned her eyes away from the window and smiled at him, "you were a very good teacher." "Does your husband?" Bill ventured. Sarah was wearing a tight fitting black cashmere turtleneck, "Steven tried…but I was the one who did most of the talking for us," and three thin silver bracelets on her left wrist, "I was just at the camera store to pick up the pictures." He rested his chin in the palm of his right hand, "So, that's what you were doing downtown." She nodded, "I work around the corner from here," leaned back in the seat, "I dropped the film off on Friday and they said it might be ready today but…" with a shrug, "I'm glad I didn't just you know," before gesturing toward the camera store on the other side of the street, "call them on the phone. If I had I would have never run into you." He glanced at the bartender, who was absorbed in his book before asking, "Do you live nearby?" "Not too far, we live over by the zoo. It's only a ten-minute drive," she enthuastically added, "I like to walk to work…when it's warm enough." Bill imagined her walking tree-lined sidewalks as the rest of the city piled into cars and raced off to work. "Do you still

16

live in Sauquoit?" "In the same house," he quietly replied, "with the same wife." Sarah lay her palms on the table, "Actually Bill," and spread her fingers apart, "I think about you all the time." He cautiously placed his hands, "Well…" on top of hers, "I've really missed you." She turned her palms over, "You were my first love," and took hold of his hands.

Monday, April 19, 1976

Bill kept Sarah after the bell to find out why she was failing his class. She dutifully asked him to recommend a senior who would be willing to tutor her. He wrote a name and number down on a scrap of orange paper then offered her a ride home.

"And the photographs," Sarah glanced at Bill, "you should see them," as they continued along the narrow path, "the models are wearing casts and some of them even have black eyes," they walked by a clump of flowering bluebells as she concluded, "it's like pornography only worse." A chipmunk scurried across a large rock then disappeared into a pile of leaves. "Women being beaten by groups of men in suits…How could anyone find that beautiful?" Bill stepped over the trunk of a tree that had fallen across the trail, "I know I don't," turned to her, and held out his right hand.

The cloudless sky was teeming with dozens of songbirds in flight. She placed her left hand in his, "it's like the feminist movement never happened," and stepped over the trunk. The plaster cast on Sarah's right arm extended from her elbow to her wrist. He stepped on a brittle weed and a cluster of brown thistles clung to the cuff of his pant leg. Laura had covered the cast in tiny red hearts and flowers with fingernail polish. When a blossoming willow caught Bill's eye, he stopped walking, "I think they've run out of supposedly wholesome ways," and pointed it out to her, "to sell expensive clothes to wealthy women." The willow's flowering limbs swayed as the breeze cast off a shower of yellow petals. "What does that say about the way society treats women?" A multitude of bees, undeterred by the breeze, pollinated the tree. "But aren't the models just well paid mannequins?" Bill realized that he was still holding her hand. She frowned, "What does that mean?" "It isn't that complicated, Sarah," beads of sweat appeared on his forehead, "the people behind the camera simply script fantasy roles for women and those roles have little or nothing to do with reality." The air around them was enriched by the scent of the blooming tree. "Well," she looked at him closely, "don't you think it says a lot about the kind of people who buy them?" and noticed the faint outline of her reflection in his brown eyes. "I suppose," he nodded, "but aren't most of those designers gay?" A robin in a nearby tree began to sing. They saw each other in class, their last class of the day, five days a week, and yet she never looked the same. He was almost twice her age, "I mean, that really doesn't have anything to do with it, but it does seem strange that you would get so worked up about advertisements in fashion magazines." She smiled tentatively at her reflection while asking, "How is it not complicated?" Bill had been married for three years, "things like that are very temporal," and he was as bored by his wife's passionless lovemaking as he was repulsed by the middle-class existence that pacified her. He was as embarrassed by his wife's ideals, "next year they'll find something else," as he was resigned to them. "Like what?" "Who knows," Bill shrugged, "maybe next year they'll use vivisection to peddle their dresses." Sarah let go of his hand, "that's very funny," and began walking away. He watched her hips sway beneath her blue jeans, "Can I ask you something?" She turned around, "you just did." He stepped toward her, "Why does that bother you so much?" She lowered her eyes, "I really thought you were different," and scratched at the rash above her cast, "So, why make jokes about something you obviously don't understand?" Her fingernails left faint whitish trails around the rash. "I was being ironic, Sarah." A bee hovered above a cluster of dandelions just inches away from the tips of her sandals. "You're being an asshole."

She told him in the car that the cast would be removed next Monday and that she was very self-conscious about the way it smelled. When asked if her parents were concerned about her grades she looked out the open window of his Impala and laughed. When asked why that was funny, she spoke enthusiastically about Truffaut's *The 400 Blows*, which he had shown the class a month ago—then made it clear to him that the only place she didn't want to go was home.

"What is it I don't understand, Sarah?" She placed her hands on her hips, "What is it you wanted to show me, Mister Richardson?" He took two steps forward, "I thought maybe we could talk and you could tell me—" "Tell you what," she held her ground, "that I'm going to love playing in your magic tree-fort?" "You can start by telling me why you're failing my class." She shrugged before looking intently above his head. He softened his tone, "There's a beautiful lake a short walk from here," then motioned toward the trail, "are you coming or not?" She nodded sullenly, and they continued along the trail. "I don't care if you call me an asshole, we can always disagree, but please don't ever call me mister." "Why not?" "Because it makes me feel like an old man." "What about Mister Asshole?" Sarah laughed. "That really doesn't work either," furrowing his brow, "I'd really like for you to think of me as a friend...okay?" She took his hand while asking, "How old are you?" "I'll be thirty-one this August." "Oh, that's right, you're a Leo...you are the most willful." "Not that nonsense again." "It's not nonsense, Bill, you can tell a lot about a person from the sign they are born under." "For instance?" "The Zodiac is how we, as mortal beings, have passed from the spirit world into the material one." Holding Sarah's hand while being lectured about the Zodiac made Bill feel like he was sixteen again. "The world is divided into two opposing parts, involution and evolution. The first six signs of the Zodiac represent involution and-" "What are the first six signs?" He asked. "Aries, Taurus, Gemini, Cancer, and then you the Leo," squeezing his hand for emphasis, "the willful lion, and then Virgo, the soulful giver." "And when were you born?" With a smile, "My birthday is in February, under the sign of Aquarius." "Isn't that a water sign?" "Aquarius is the water bearer, but it's actually an air sign, it's the eleventh sign in the Zodiac, on the side of evolution. Aquarius symbolizes the disintegration of existing forms. It's a symbol of liberation." Bill's foot got caught on a root and he almost tripped. "Be careful there..." he nodded sheepishly as she continued, "The Egyptians identified Aquarius with their god Hapi who personified the Nile and when it flooded it was a tremendous source of both agricultural and spiritual importance." He was tempted to suggest that if she spent half as much time studying French as she did astrology then she wouldn't be failing his class. They passed a rusting black and white sign nailed to a tree, warning trespassers they would be prosecuted. "So," Sarah concluded, "we are from opposite sides of the Zodiac and I think that is a very good thing." The trail opened onto a small clearing. "And you consider yourself," they startled a pair of mourning doves foraging in the tall grass, "a liberated person?" their wings made an airy whistling sound as they flew away. "I do," with a solemn nod, "to the extent that a woman can be in a society that is dominated by men." He turned to her, "And how much of that has to do with the sign you are born under?" She said, "Everything," with conviction. "Come on, Sarah, don't you think your environment has more to do with shaping the person you are and the one you'll turn out to be?" "No, I don't," she stopped walking, "I think it's the other way around," and let go of his hand. "It's all up to your astrological sign?" "You know," she noted his smirk, "arrogance is another one of the Leo's traits." He placed his hands on his waist, "It seems to me you've got it all backwards." "How so?" A crow cawed as it flew above the meadow. He looked away from her before asking, "How did you break your arm?" "I fell off my bike," she bit her lower lip, "I told you that." He frowned, "Yes, you did." She looked down at the clump of green grass between them, "So how far away is this world famous lake of yours?" He nodded in the direction they'd been walking, "It's just beyond this meadow." She tried to sound apathetic, "Are we going there or not?" He cleared his throat before stating, "The most important virtue in any relationship is honesty." She stepped toward him, "You are nothing like any of my other teachers." "I think most of your teachers are in school because of the paycheck they get every other Friday." She nodded, "It is so easy to talk to you." "If they had to sell shoes instead of teaching to pay the bills, it wouldn't faze them one bit." Her curly blonde locks, "Everyone in class thinks you're really cool," were rearranged in the breeze. He glanced at her chest, "It is very important to me that we are always honest with each other." Her dark brown nipples were erect and visible through the light cotton blouse. "Sure, Bill." He scratched the top of his head, "I'm really glad you feel that way, Sarah," and looked down at her sandals, "let's not keep any secrets from each other." Her toes were perfectly symmetrical and the nails were dark red. "Sure Bill, I think honesty—" "I think you already know that I really care about you," he looked into her eyes, "and I always want you to tell me the truth." Her smile, "Sure," revealed the narrow gap between her two front teeth. "Don't you have a boyfriend?" "No, I did," shaking her head, "but he broke up with me right before Christmas." "Did he hurt you?" The trees cast long shadows around the edge of the meadow. "Not really, he was a real jerk though. I still don't know why I went out with him." "No," Bill shook his head, "I meant physically," while looking at her intently, "Did he break your arm?" "No way," her eyes widened, "I don't like guys like that…jocks or violent ones." A jet silently streaked across the blue sky leaving a thin contrail behind. "What kind of guys do you like?" She began to blush, "Older ones, I guess, most of the guys my age are so immature…they behave like little kids." "What about married men?" She laughed out loud. "Why is that so funny?" The last thing she wanted to do was offend him, "it's not," but he had such a constipated expression on his face, "you make it sound so serious," she took hold of his left hand and examined the gold band, "aren't you married?" He nodded before she added, "I've even met your wife." Bill slowly pulled his hand away, "When?" "She's almost as tall as me and she has long brown hair and," Sarah winked, "and her name is Mary." "How do you know her name?" She felt like a lawyer on television presenting a surprise witness to a stunned jury, "Mary chaperoned a dance in my sophomore year," with a giggle, "you're not very *happily* married to Mary though." "Sarah," he began to blush, "I asked you a question and I'd like for you to answer it." She held up her left hand, "Okay," and whispered an oath, "I've never dated a married man," before placing her left hand on his shoulder and kissing him on the mouth, "but in twenty years you'll still be fourteen years older than me."

Friday, March 28, 1997 Part 1

Sarah contemplated his tranquil expression before saying, "I always thought you had," in a soft voice. Bill pulled the damp condom off his flaccid erection, "that isn't true." The pounding in his chest had begun to subside. Sarah possessed a glowing intensity that radiated between them, "A lot of girls in school," her cheeks were a rosy pink, "said they slept with you," and her eyes were wide open. Sperm collected in the tip of the condom he held between the thumb and forefinger of his right hand. She pressed her thighs together and sighed. He weighed the fluid with an absentminded pride, "That certainly doesn't mean I did." A television could be heard through the wall behind the bed. She reached behind her back with both hands and undid the tangled clasp of her bra. He leaned over and placed the condom in the ashtray. She pulled the black bra away from her breasts and cast it onto the edge of the bed. To the right of the ashtray there was a beige touch-tone phone. "How could you believe something like that was true?" To the right of the phone, a red and white brochure instructed the occupants on how to exit the building in the event of a fire. A metal lamp with a beige lampshade was mounted to the wall above the nightstand; a sixty-watt bulb illuminated a portion of the room. She waited for him to adjust the thin foam pillow beneath his head before claiming, "Because you never took me seriously." Long brown watermarks ran across the ceiling above the bed. He closed his eyes, "That isn't true," clasped his hands and rested them on his stomach.

Bill had saved a batch of color photographs of Sarah from the spring of '76 and would remove them from the cardboard box marked *poetry* that was buried in the bottom of the closet in his study at least twice every five years. Mary would be spending the weekend at her sister's in Bridgeport, and he would be home alone and very drunk. Bill and Sarah had driven up to Sylvan Beach on a sunny weekday during the Easter break of her junior year. The image of Sarah standing on the beach with her jeans rolled up to her knees as small waves broke before her pale ankles. The image of Sarah feeding a seagull (with outstretched wings) French fries while sitting at a dark red picnic bench. The portrait of her looking directly into the fifty-millimeter lens—her blue eyes almost mirrored the cloudless sky. Sarah sitting on the back of a green bench overlooking Oneida Lake. Sarah holding a melting chocolate ice cream cone with a sardonic grin. Bill would spend hours pouring over the images until he was seeing double.

The springs in the mattress creaked, "Like you were just testing the bath water with the tip of your foot," as she placed her right arm on his chest. He opened his eyes, "What does that mean?" The television situated on the dresser parallel to the bed reflected their faint silhouettes in its darkened screen. She noticed the crow's feet, "that you were just interested in having sex with me," etched around the corners of his eyes, "and that you just saw me as some dumb, needy girl—" "How can you—" he tried to interject. "Who really couldn't give you anything else." "You were sixteen years old," Bill shook his head while adding, "and I couldn't believe how lucky I was to have found someone who was as…as passionately interested in me as you were then," then lowered his voice, "it was like a dream come true," as the realization that it had taken two decades to tell her this descended upon him. "You never made me feel like you were committed to our relationship." "I certainly tried," he nodded with conviction, "the sex was very important, the sex was incredible, as it should be in every relationship, although it never is…but we shared a lot of the same interests as well." Her eyes narrowed, "You never made me feel appreciated." That she would berate him about the way their relationship ended didn't come as a surprise, "I think that had a lot more to do with your upbringing and besides—" "I always felt like you were taking me for granted," she pursed her lips, "like that letter you gave me." "Twenty years ago," he shrugged his shoulders, "you can't change the past, so why live in it?" Wasn't renewing their relationship a way of reliving the past? Televised laughter could be heard through the wall as she thought about his question. How could she have harbored his betrayal for twenty years?

The rain had finally let up by the time she reached their gravel driveway. A silver Buick was parked next to Mary's dark green Plymouth. The wind had pasted dozens of young leaves onto the sides of the cars. Water ran along the gutters and down the spouts. Her shoulder brushed the corner of the house as she walked into the backyard.

Sarah took her arm off his chest and sat up, "You know I kept it." Bill looked puzzled, "Kept what?" "That letter you gave me on the last day of school," Sarah rested her shoulders against the headboard. "Oh that," he contemplated their reflection in the television screen. "Oh that," she placed the tip of her index finger on her chin, "I should have brought it tonight," while watching his expression turn sullen, "Do you remember that day?" He nodded, "I don't remember what I wrote in it though." "You don't?" "No of course not...Jesus Christ...not word for word." She saw herself sprinting through the teacher's parking lot, "I guess you've done it before," and reached his car just as he was turning the key in the ignition. She was about to ask him what was wrong, "it was in the parking lot," as he rolled down the window, "on the last day of school," and shoved the envelope into her hands. He noticed the burgundy lipstick, "Yes," smudged around the corners of her mouth, "I do remember that." "I'll have to show it to you sometime, maybe that will refresh your memory." Bill recalled how idiotic it felt waking up with a hangover on the daybed in his study, to discover those photographs scattered across his desk. "What good would that do?" Ignoring his question, "I walked over to your house that night in the rain and you were sitting on the couch getting drunk with Mary and some other couple," while looking closely at his eyes, "I stood outside on your patio by the window and all of you seemed so old and decrepit then, so, *adult*...the way anyone over thirty looks to a teenager...all of you belonged in a mausoleum." He added, "And the girls in school are getting younger every year," with wistful irony.

"And how did we get on this subject anyway," a male voice interjected. Two rectangles of bright yellow light covered the patio. "We were toasting Brezhnev." Bill's voice washed over Sarah as she quickly moved to the wall next to the windows. "When you were in the bathroom!" A peal of drunken laughter erupted in the living room. Sarah pressed her back to the damp bricks. "Yeah, honey," a woman's shrill pitch, "we had to wait for you to leave the room." The objects surrounding Sarah gradually became visible. "To the new Soviet president!" She winced at the sound of Mary's voice. "And head of the Communist Party," Bill chimed in. The terra cotta planters by her feet were splattered with mud and filled with shallow puddles. "Who happens to be a few months away from certain death." A large brass ashtray filled with partially submerged cigarette butts. The sound of ice cubes in the bottom of a glass. "Can someone please explain the logic of that decision?" The other male voice asked. A metal watering can with a long spout. Bill said, "I'm sure that when he kicks off you'll get the call up from the Kremlin." Sarah took a deep breath and looked in the window. Mary raised her glass in a toast, "To comrade Dan," the balding man with a thick moustache sitting in the rocking chair with his legs crossed, "the next head of the Soviet State and the first Republican member of the Communist Party." Mary was lying on the couch with her stockinged feet in Bill's lap. "Well," Bill took a sip of his drink before saying, "if the Mets don't trade him to Cincinnati first." Dan looked into his empty glass and frowned, "I am not a Republican." Mary squealed with laughter, "And you're not a very good pitcher either!" Dan began rocking back and forth in his chair like an excited chimp, "I am not a Republican, nor a card carrying member of the Communist Party, nor the John Birch Society for that matter," he straightened out his legs and stood on unsteady feet, "and if the politburo approves we can drive down there tonight," before crossing to the liter of Cutty Sark and ice bucket on top of the counter, "and embrace our revolutionary brothers and soul sisters," beneath the mirror parallel to the window. He examined himself in the mirror, "who are just trying to eat their raw," twisting the metal cap off the bottle, "homegrown vegetables in peace," and pouring three fingers into his glass, "down there in the big bad city of brotherly love," before discovering Sarah's reflection in the mirror and spilling scotch all over the counter. "We were talking about adultery," Bill exclaimed. "No," the overweight woman interjected, "we were talking about books about adultery." Dan turned toward them while wiping the liquor off his hands with a green and red napkin, "How about the open one about people looking in your window?" They turned to Dan as he pointed, "I mean the book about that one in the window." Sarah ducked away and bolted across the deck. Bill stood up and stumbled toward the window. She ran through the backyard and disappeared into the shadows surrounding their property.

"For years I thought it could have been, that it *should* have been me, sitting in there with you. The happy young housewife with her husband, the brilliant teacher." Bill shrugged, "I'm sure that you can find a lot of faults with anyone in retrospect." "And I would get so angry with myself for wanting that life with you," she brushed his right hand off of her thigh, "you had convinced me that you didn't love her and I gave myself to you…unconditionally… and there you were—" "I think you were being delusional," Bill unclenched his fists, "I was never going to leave Mary," before changing the subject, "What happened with your parents?" Sarah swallowed hard, "My mother is in a nursing home and I haven't spoken to my father in thirteen years." A door down the hall slammed. "Really?" She leveled her eyes at him, "If anyone hurt Kate the way he hurt me I would kill them." "And no jury would ever convict you," he cleared his throat before adding, "what if you got pregnant in high school." "I wanted that life with you so badly," she hadn't taken her eyes off his chest, "and I…" "What then Sarah," he pressed his hands in hers, "what sort of life would we be living now?" "And I…" she blinked twice while looking intently at his face, "and I've never loved anyone the way I loved you. Not even my husband," she squeezed his hands, "even when things were really good between us. I've compared every man I've been involved with to you and none of them have even come close." He leaned forward, "I'm right here," and kissed her on the forehead. "I had an affair," she turned her head away, "with my boss." "The dentist?" She nodded, "At one point he wanted to leave his wife and kids for me and I told him I would quit and end our relationship if he even suggested it again." "How long did this go on for?" "The other night I realized I was never really able to love any of them…it was more like a role I was playing," she cleared her throat, "after we ran into each other last month I ended it with him." Bill managed to mask his skepticism, "Just like that," but how many hours had she spent with her boss in a room like this, "you didn't know," he swallowed dryly, "you didn't know that we would be intimate again?" "That didn't matter," she leaned forward, "knowing that you still cared about me was enough," and kissed him on the mouth.

Friday, June 25, 1976

A warm breeze parted the drawn yellow curtain as it entered her bedroom. *Mon Amour Bill,* Her blue eyes followed the black lines across the page *It has already been eight days since I last saw you* of loose-leaf paper she held in her left hand *and the time away from you has been so hard. If you had a picture of me right now you would see me lying on my bed looking at your picture in the yearbook.* Her head was resting on two pillows. *I am wearing the shirt you gave me and a denim skirt.* Sunlight fell upon a portion of the hardwood floor. *I wish I had a better picture of you. I let you take so many pictures of me and the only one I have of you is the crappy one in the yearbook that doesn't even look like you.* The radio on the dresser was playing quietly. *Not that photographs are all that important it's just that I miss you so much. Missing you like this makes me feel like there is this heavy weight on my chest.* A group of sparrows was chirping outside the window. *Almost like I can't breathe. I feel so alone now that it almost seems unreal.* Three daisies in a Coke bottle half-filled with cloudy water on the dresser next to the radio. *You know that the time I spend in your arms or walking by your side feels like the most amazing thing I have ever experienced.* She raised her legs and placed her bare feet on the lemon yellow bedspread. *I spent today in my room listening to the radio and thinking about what is going on in my life right now.* The curtain fell back into place. *In a way things seem to have changed so much in just eight days and there are times when the distance between us just gets stronger and it feels like every hour we can't see each other this wall growing between us just gets higher.* Her mother coughed while walking past the bedroom door. *Not being able to at least talk to you or hear the sound of your voice has been so hard for me.* She turned the page over. *Mom is in the living room watching her soaps it's so annoying because it's so loud she is almost completely deaf. My dad finally found a job so he isn't home during the day and things are a lot calmer around here now.* She took the pen off the bed *I hope you are doing okay and Mary isn't driving you completely crazy* placed the paper on her left leg and drew a wavy black line through the last four sentences. *I wonder how different this summer would be if we had gone to France together?* The thought of having lunch with Bill while sitting outside a quaint café made her smile. *She couldn't possibly appreciate the person you really are in the thousands of ways that I do.* Sarah crossed out *She* and wrote *Mary* then read the next line. *I want so much to call you right now or to be held in your arms because what I have to tell you isn't very easy and I really hope this letter doesn't make you too disappointed in me and you don't get upset but I feel like I need to be with someone over the summer.* She wrote *for me* above *easy* and then reread the sentence three times. *I don't know why it's so important for me to be with someone or how this time away from you can be so painful but it is so this is what is happening right now.* The guitar solo on the radio faded into a car commercial. *You* underlined twice *said we can't see each other again until school starts in September even after you return from France and I met this guy at a party last weekend and I really like him.* She began to wonder how Bill would react when he received this letter. *He's smart and funny he's a year older than me and he just graduated.* She recalled Robert's diligent hands between her thighs and down the front pockets of her jeans and clutched the bedspread between her toes. *I just want you to know that I still love you very much and if we could see each other over the summer then you know I would not be doing this.* A warm breeze parted the curtain as it entered her bedroom. *And that is why it has been so hard for me to be away from you. If only we could see each other right now even from a distance. It has been impossible for me to write you this because it makes me feel like I have given up on us and I have failed our love.* Sunlight briefly fell upon a portion of the hardwood floor. *It's a crazy love that we share but I think* She placed the page on her leg, pressed the pen to the page then crossed out *think* and wrote *hope*. The telephone in the kitchen rang. *you understand that I still love you and that to be loved by you is a very special thing and I'm not doing this to make you jealous and I* She crossed out *I* and wrote *you*. The telephone rang again. *you always say that honesty is the most important part of any relationship.* She considered returning Robert's call and wondered if that was who had just called. *So if you see me around this summer and I am with somebody it is probably him and please just remember that I couldn't possibly love him as much as I do you.* Her mother knocked. She folded the letter in half and then tore it in two. "Honey the phone," her mother called through the door, "it's that boy again." Sarah swung her legs off the bed and crossed to the door while tearing the letter again. Her mother said, "Your new friend is on the phone," as Sarah opened the door, "you should at least talk to him...sleeping beauty." Sarah clutched the letter in her fist, "Okay mom," and ducked around her. "I hope you aren't planning on spending the entire summer in your bedroom," the soles of her bare feet padded across the peeling linoleum, "because the whole world is out there just waiting to be discovered," as she walked to the telephone.

Friday, March 28, 1997 *Part 2*

Bill thought of taking her picture as she stood on the shore of Sylvan Beach. Sarah had removed her sneakers and socks, rolled up her jeans, and stepped into the dark gray water. "It's sooo fucking cold!" He was standing five yards away when he framed her in the viewfinder and focused. She looked down at the miniature waves breaking around her ankles just before he took the picture.

"Why were you playing a role?" Bill asked. Sarah's shoulders were covered with gooseflesh, "I guess in some stupid way I felt that if I couldn't be fulfilled by one person then two might make me feel," she stopped herself from saying happy, "the thing is I could never convince myself that it was true." He shifted on the bed, "That what was true?" She frowned, "That I was unhappy," shrugging her shoulders, "or I was just really lonely," then looked closely at his face, "or maybe I had finally convinced myself things would never change and I would never have another chance with you." Bill examined their entwined fingers, "When did you start sleeping with your boss?" comparing their mismatched wedding bands. "In December." "That wasn't very long ago," he sighed, "you made it sound like—" "December of '94," she bit her lower lip, "it was three years ago…right after I started taking Prozac." "And you're still working there?" When she smiled and said, "I just got a raise," he noticed how white her teeth were. He took his hands away and stood up. "Where are you going?" He stood on the gray carpet, "To the bathroom," and crossed the room.

Dearest Sarah, She saw him in the teacher's parking lot and ran over to his car. *We have had the very real pleasure of each other's company for more than a year now, but this relationship cannot continue any longer.* She got there just as he was turning the key in the ignition and breathlessly asked, "What's the matter with you?" *I know this will not be easy for you to understand and it wasn't easy for me to reach this decision but I need you to be strong for me and for yourself.* He rolled down the window and gave her the letter. *I have carefully thought through the plans we have made and the dreams we share for our life together and I honestly feel that I will be nothing more than a blight on your future.* When she asked what was wrong, he replied, "I think it's time to move on." *The love and passion we have shared has been a real blessing and you have helped me rediscover a part of my youth that I thought I had lost forever.* "What," she pressed her hands on the car door, "what are you talking about?" *I am ashamed to admit that I could never be willing or able to leave my wife for you.* He revved the engine while asking, "How is this being discreet?" *And instead of living a lie that would have only created greater unhappiness for us in the future I think it's best we come to our senses now and honor the secret love and friendship we have shared.* The car pulled away as she stood there. *I will never forget you and I will always be devoted to the memory of our time together.*

With much love and gratitude,

Bill

40

She was smoking when he returned. "Does it bother you that I'm on anti-depressants?" He stood at the end of the bed, "Isn't everyone in America on Prozac?" She exhaled, "I'm being serious," while scrutinizing his torso. "Well," shifting his feet, "is it helping?" She said, "Sometimes," before placing the cigarette between her lips. "Then it doesn't bother me," the mattress sagged beneath him, "I didn't know that you smoked," as he sat next to her. "Maybe a pack every other week," she noticed a tiny bit of flesh-colored wax on his earlobe, "why were you looking at me like," picked it off with her index fingernail and flicked it onto the floor, "like you were afraid of me." Bill shrugged, "Did you hear about that cult in California?" Their clothes had slipped off the back of the wooden chair and formed a pile on the floor. "Heavens Gate?" The smoke from her cigarette swirled above the lampshade. He nodded, "It was all over the news again tonight." She cleared her throat, "They thought the comet was coming to take their souls away," and placed the cigarette between her lips. "And maybe it did," he turned to her, "you know it's flying above our heads right now." She exhaled slowly, "Hale-Bopp," and the smoke was pushed beneath the lampshade, "that is just so sad," where it lingered in the yellow light, "they claimed their bodies were only temporary vehicles holding in their souls and when Kate and I saw that clip on the news she said all of those bodies, the way they were all dressed up in those uniforms, made them look like envelopes." "I really loved you, Sarah." Her eyes were downcast, "Then why did you end it?" Bill shook his head while saying, "I wasn't." She reached over and crushed the cigarette in the ashtray, "You used me." "That was twenty years ago." She crossed her arms beneath her breasts, "Can't you just apologize for hurting me?"

"Why have you victimized yourself over this?"

Clenching her jaw, "I want to know why you took me for granted."

"The risks were just impossible."

She placed her hands on her knees, "Just tell me why you gave up on us."

"Answer my question."

"It's not like I could have gotten pregnant anyway," she looked at him uneasily, "I was on the pill....Remember? That was your idea."

He nodded, "Weren't you on the pill in college?"

The off-handed way she said, "I really wanted to have your baby," stunned him. Bill shook his head in disbelief, "I wouldn't have given you that choice." "You're an idiot," she looked away, "I wanted to spend my life with you." "That's not what I thought was best for you," he examined the tufts of hair below his knuckles, "that was a mistake on my part, a selfish and—" "Is this a mistake?" "No," he didn't hesitate, "no, it isn't." She stretched her long legs out on the bedspread, "I'm going to see you again?" He nodded before asking, "If we had married, do you think we would still be happy?" "Why," she placed her hands on his shoulders, "wouldn't we be happy now?" and kissed him on the cheek. He closed his eyes before saying, "That's an interesting question."

Saturday, March 19, 1977

The bus pulled away, leaving a haze of diesel fumes behind. Laura stepped over a heap of blackened snow. "Are you sure?" They walked by a bright red fire hydrant. The logo on the rear of the bus *We're here to get you there* was coated with a grainy film of black exhaust. Low clouds extended across the sky. Laura continued, "Or are you just telling me something you think I want to hear?" in the same aggressive tone she had been using for the entire ride back from Utica. Trails of half-dissolved rock salt ran along the cracks in the sidewalk. An orange patch of sun hung beneath a canopy of dark grey clouds. "No," Sarah's breath was visible in the frigid air, "that's just what he said." Laura was carrying a blue and white plastic shopping bag under her left arm, "When?" The bag contained a second hand black turtleneck and a plaid wool skirt. The sidewalk ended at the corner, mounds of brown snow lined the sides of the road. "Just the other night."

Mary had crept downstairs around midnight while Bill and Sarah were in his study. She knocked on the door and Sarah had just enough time to squeeze between the daybed and the wall before Mary turned the knob and pushed open the door, "Honey, are you awake?" "I am now," Bill cleared his throat before asking, "What is it?" Mary turned on the overhead light and stood there in her pink flannel nightgown, "Bill," blinking in the doorway, "come to bed." He covered his waist with a wool blanket, "What's the matter?" "You said you weren't going to do this anymore." Sarah's heart was pounding in her constricting chest. Bill rubbed his eyes, "Go back upstairs," and yawned before saying, "I'll be right there."

The bare trees hung in the twilight without casting shadows on the lawns. Laura said, "Yeah, well." The streetlight came on as they walked beneath it. "Yeah, well what?" Sarah was thinking about how distant Bill was to her in class the next day. "Are you sure," dark orange freckles covered Laura's pale face, "that's exactly what he said?" and her long red hair was carried away from her shoulders by the wind. "Maybe," Sarah was wearing her navy pea coat, "but not in so many words," blue jeans, a beige wool hat and a pair of black high tops. The library copy of *Alice in Wonderland* was tucked beneath her left arm. A car with a hole in its muffler drove by. Sarah buried her hands deeper into her pockets. Every time they saw each other, Laura reproached her for not spending as much time together as they'd used to. The wind was cutting into their backs. "I just don't see how he would be that committed to you." They walked by a snowman leaning over a sled. "How can you say that?" "Because it sounds like he's just telling you whatever it is you want to hear." "That just isn't true." Another car drove by. Laura took a pack of cigarettes out of her coat pocket, "But you told me," and removed one from the pack, "he's done it with a lot of other girls," hunched her shoulders to block the wind and lit it with a small green disposable lighter. "That was a long time ago." She took the cigarette from her mouth and exhaled, "That was last month, Sarah." "Maybe I don't want to think that way anymore." The more time they spent away from each other, "He

44

probably told them all the same thing," the more selective Laura's memory became, "that he loves them," she rolled her eyes, "so they won't go and tell the principal when he dumps them after he gets tired of fucking them." "I think I was just being paranoid." "If he does *love you*," Laura shook her head, "then why is he so worried about losing his job?" "Because he wouldn't be able to teach anymore. Bill loves me and he tells me that all the time." "That is just another name for it." "For what?" "For you being a completely brainwashed idiot," Laura had been listening to how great Bill was all afternoon. Sarah thought of all the guys Laura slept with and how she constantly bragged about not caring for any of them, "How can *you* say that?" "Because when you love someone you would be willing to do anything to be with them," she put her hands on her hips, "regardless of what people think or what they say. When I fall in love," pointing at herself with the two fingers holding the cigarette, "that's the way it has to be…all or nothing…otherwise, I'll know I'm not in love." Sarah smirked, "All or nothing?" "Exactly. That's the way it's going to be." They walked in silence for another ten yards before Laura quietly asked, "What do you want to do tonight?" Before Bill came along, they'd planned on attending college together. She shrugged, "I really don't care." Laura had been accepted to Syracuse University on a partial scholarship, and Sarah had yet to fill out a single application. "We could go to the bowling alley?" Sarah though of partying in the parking lot, "Yuck." "If my brother is around, he'll give us a ride…" Laura laughed, "as long as you sit in the front seat with him." She shook her head, "No." "Come on, it'll be fun." Sarah wanted to spend the night with Bill, "It doesn't sound like *fun*," but they never saw each other on the weekends anymore, "it sounds like a waste of time," because he said it was dangerous. "He's turning you into an old lady," Laura's house was identical to the three other split-level houses along the cul-de-sac, "my mom is going to be so happy to see you." Her brother's green Dodge Dart was parked in the driveway. "Where is your dad?" "He's working nights on the weekends now." The streetlight went out as they walked beneath it. "That's too bad," Sarah said. Laura laughed, "You really do have a thing for married men."

Sunday, April 20, 1997

They arrived at the nursery just as it opened and purchased the cherry tree Mary had reserved last Thursday. Bill secured the tree in the open trunk of their Jetta. Mary anxiously claimed that the blossoms would be blown off as they drove home. He insisted the tree wouldn't fit in the backseat and they needed to rush home and plant it before the forecasted rain began.

Bill dug the hole while Mary removed the tree from the planter, shook off the dark soil clinging to the roots and inspected them. He jabbed the spade into the sides of the hole to loosen the soil. She pruned back the damaged roots with shears. He chopped up the sod and shoveled it into the hole as clouds darkened the sky. She spread compost around the roots as he held the tree upright. She filled in the hole and leveled the subsoil. He collected two wooden stakes, a mallet, and a ball of heavy twine from the garage. He pounded the stakes into the soil, and she tied them to the narrow trunk. It began to rain and she realized they'd forgotten to cover the bottom of the hole with gravel. He assured her it wasn't necessary before returning the tools to the garage.

Mary thought of the conversation they'd had in the car while filling the kettle with cold water. She finally asked why he was spending so many nights sleeping in his study. He gripped the steering wheel and clenched his jaw. She also wanted to know why he was so impatient with her. He muttered an apology and claimed he was under a lot of stress and it was aggravated by the fact that he hadn't been sleeping well. He went on to explain that stress was self-perpetuating as was the insomnia that accompanied it. Mary offered to help him. Bill shook his head, "I was thinking about going away," then glanced at her out of the corner of his eye, "by myself for a few days." Her look of dismay, "Alone?" He kept his eyes on the road, "Yes," and tried to sound nonchalant, "over Memorial Day weekend." "Without me," she cleared her throat, "why?" "To relax and," Bill paused long enough to gauge her response, "and sort a few things out." She tugged at the shoulder strap of her seatbelt, "Like what sort of things?" When he didn't respond she frowned, "What's been bothering you?" He sighed, "I don't know if…" while entertaining the idea of telling her the truth. Her eyes narrowed, "You don't know, if what?" Bill wondered if he was actually in love with Sarah as he said, "How to articulate it." She sank back in the passenger seat, "Are you depressed?" The car sped by a recently plowed field. He decided that love *could* be the right word to describe his feelings, "I think I could be." She clasped her hands, "Perhaps you should talk to someone about it," and looked out the window as the telephone poles flashed past, "instead of just running away by yourself." He realized that his foot was nearly flat on the gas pedal, "I think I, " that the car was going 85, "I just need some time to myself," and eased his foot off the gas, "I should be able to work it out alone."

Friday, October 22, 1976

"People need illusions," the candle projected flickering shadows on the ceiling, "it gives them a sense of security." She nodded, "People get married because of fear." They were lying on his daybed. "Vulnerability and fear are two very different things." The flame wavered in the draft. "How so?" Bill wrapped his arms around her waist, "Fear is very temporary," she reveled in his warmth, "yet vulnerability is permanent," and the sound of his voice, "Sarah." She felt so diminutive in his arms when he said her name. The hands of the oval desk clock indicated the correct time. "Then why did you get married?" He hesitated before saying, "I got married because I fell in love." It was two-fifteen. She calculated the time it would take her to walk home, "isn't that an illusion as well," they had almost two more hours. The patchwork quilt they were entwined beneath had a fan pattern, "It didn't seem like that at the time," and had been made the previous winter by his wife. She pressed her hips into his, "What about now?" He thought about Mary who was upstairs, "And now you're here," and the sleeping pills she took every night. "It's so hard for me to imagine that you were ever happy together,"

Sarah didn't want to sound possessive but she wanted to suggest that they get a divorce, while watching the thin red second hand on the clock move from one to seven. It got all the way to eleven, and she still hadn't come up with a tactful way of saying it. The flame grew an inch as it flickered back and forth. Sarah thought of Mary toiling in her garden during the spring and summer. Mary's slender fingers deftly pulling weeds out of her meticulously crafted flowerbeds. Mary hunched over her sewing machine all winter long. Mary's fingers skillfully guiding the needle through the dotted lines of the latest McCall's dress pattern with her thin bloodless lips pursed in concentration. Mary was the perfectly frigid wife who wore a hand-made apron while baking sheet-cakes for PTA functions. Everything she did was just so perfectly prefabricated—like a Sears catalog model. Walter, the fifteen-pound tabby, sat up on his hind legs at the edge of the daybed and began licking his belly. Sarah smiled as the cat began to purr. "Why do you think your parents got married?" Looking up from the cat, "Because my father needed a slow-moving punching bag." "Do you think they've ever been happy?" Bill didn't wait for Sarah to reply, "they've never been happy together because happiness was never their priority. Their generation pursued an illusion of family because that's how they were conditioned." "My parents might have been happy together," Sarah had worn a cast on her left arm during the late winter, "when they were younger," and early spring of her junior year, "like when my mother gave birth to more punching bags." She told everyone at school an elaborate lie about falling off her bike after skidding on a patch of ice and nearly getting run over by a car. She told Bill the truth after they had sex for the first time in the back seat of his car. "You can always stay here if it gets that bad again. I'll just tell Mary you're one of my best students and you're having problems at home." "Really?" Sarah whispered. He kissed her on the nape of her neck, "She'll understand." She tried to imagine what living with him would be like, "That is so sweet of you," and began to blush. "Then you'll be able to sleep in this room." "I don't know," it sounded too good to be true, "seeing you with her all the time would make me so crazy." Massaging her shoulders, "That way we could spend every night together without you having to crawl in and out of your," she turned to face him, "bedroom window like a cat burglar," and he discovered her warm smile. She looked at his eyes, "don't you think that would make a good poem," before kissing him on the lips. "I think that poem has already been written." She kissed him again, "But not written nearly as well as you could do," before rolling on top of him.

Sarah stepped through thin pockets of ice while making her way over the ditch. The sound punctuated the silence. The cold air clung to her face and her breath was visible. Streams of grey clouds were pushed across the sky, revealing and obscuring the silver crescent of the moon. Her hands were buried in the pockets of her coat. She looked back when she reached the road. His study was dark—she blinked twice—the candle was out. The wind in her face caused her eyes to tear. Shivering as she turned and walked away from his house. The broken yellow line in the center of the road was still visible. A spray of snow was blowing between her sneakers as the wind pushed at her back. It was a three-mile walk.

She pressed her eyes closed and felt her heart beating rapidly in her head. Wrapping her fingers around his wrist, she discovered their hearts were beating in unison, "Do you think it's still snowing?" The sound of the wind on the window had died. "It wasn't snowing very hard before." They listened to the silence for a long moment before he whispered, "It's so quiet outside." She nodded,

"Winter is here." "We'll get a dusting of snow," clearing his throat, "nothing more than an inch." She looked at the clock on his desk, "I should leave soon," it was three. He frowned, "Not right now?" "Pretty soon." Bill sighed, "it's almost impossible for me to fall asleep after you leave," as she placed her head on his chest. She closed her eyes and imagined they were lying on an open raft that was floating across the ocean; gulls wheeled overhead as dolphins leapt out of the sea. Sarah opened her eyes, "It's a long walk." He kissed her forehead, "I'd like to make love to you again before you leave." She placed her hands between his thighs, "Alright," caressing his erection, "but the time goes by so quickly when we do that."

A plowed field partially covered in a thin coating of snow. The upturned soil ran like parallel black lines alongside the white rows. Icicles clinging to the underside of the telephone wires broke off in a gust of wind and shattered on the ground. She thought of the argument they'd had while she'd been getting dressed and frowned. Why was it so important for him to know how she'd lost her virginity? Why hadn't she invented another story? She realized that when she'd said, Men lie to get what they want and then they leave, it could apply to him as well. She suspected that he slept with a lot of girls who'd taken his class—they flocked around him—especially the older ones. If something like this was happening to her, surely it had happened with a lot of other girls. She looked up at the sound of an approaching milk truck and jumped the ditch before its headlights illuminated the road. She ran to a nearby oak, crouched behind the trunk, and watched the elongated reflection of the tree flash by on the side of the stainless steel tank. She waited until the taillights disappeared around a bend before standing up.

"Well Sarah," he placed the thumb and forefinger of his right hand beneath her chin and smiled, "I don't think we would be together if I weren't one of your teachers." She looked deeply into his eyes, "I knew you were going to say that." "How did you know?" Taking his right hand, "I have ways of reading your mind," and kissing the tips of his fingers. He placed his left hand on her stomach, "It was a very good question." She drew closer, "And?" Resting his palm on her pubic hair, "Why do you need to know?" She opened her legs, "I need to know everything about you because I love you," to accommodate his fingers, "I could never imagine anything like this happening to me in a million years." He wrapped his right arm around her shoulders, "So how did you know that was what I was thinking about?" She bit her lower lip, "About what a beautiful mouth I have." The sound of the wind in the pines as a draft passed through the window. "You know I love you so much." The flame flickered in the draft. He nodded while saying, "Nobody would understand what we share." "Just don't look at me that way in class and they won't." "I don't think anyone in school would have the wherewithal to know what's going on. You give your classmates too much credit." "You think so?" "They've never had to pay the slightest bit of attention to what is going on around them, so why would they start now?" "We had to write an essay today…I mean yesterday, in English for current events. And I wrote about that ferry that capsized on the Mississippi and how reading about it in the newspaper affected my life." Walter sat facing them on the center of the circular rug. Bill said, "I heard about that. Fifty people died—" "It was really sad. They say most of the people were sleeping in their cars when it capsized." "Have you taken a look at that list of colleges I gave you last week?" She lowered her eyes, "Did you hear about that cargo ship that disappeared in the Bermuda Triangle?" "No I didn't." She kissed him on the mouth,

"The Sylvia L. Ossa vanished without a trace." "Very mysterious," Bill added. Kissing him again, "Isn't that a pretty name though?" He nodded, "I'd like to have a ship named after me." She began to giggle, "Not if it's going to vanish in the Bermuda Triangle."

Sarah walked toward the picnic bench beneath her bedroom window. Snow had melted into her sneakers and it felt like her socks had frozen to her toes. She stepped onto the bench and looked into her bedroom. Her breath created a slight haze on the glass. There was no light shining beneath the bedroom door. Her parents were still upstairs, asleep. She placed her hands on the bottom of the window and pushed it up an inch. The casements had been coated with soap. She slipped her fingers beneath the window and pushed it open very slowly. She placed her right leg over the ledge and stepped into her bedroom.

"How old were you when you lost your virginity?" Sarah frowned, "That's an embarrassing question." "You said you were going to tell me tonight." Rolling off of him and onto her side, "Do you really want to hear about this?" He nodded, "I do." She sat up and placed her shoulders on the upholstered headrest. "Why is that so important to you?" The fabric had a decorative floral pattern. Resting his head on a pillow, "What happened?" She spread her fingers out and ran them through her hair a half-dozen times before asking, "Do you really want to know?" He nodded, "If you want to tell me, yes. Although I don't think I've ever forced you to do anything you didn't want to." "It was after my cousin's wedding in Syracuse," she sighed, "the reception was at this restaurant and everyone got really drunk, everyone was dancing." "How old were you?" She looked at him cautiously, "Thirteen." He nodded, "And you were drinking?" "I snuck a couple glasses of champagne,

I really don't like the taste of it." "Maybe when you're older," he suggested, "it's an acquired taste." "And I was dancing with a friend of the groom." "How old was he?" "He said he was twenty-five," she looked at the frost coating the window, "we were dancing and then I had to pee because of the champagne and he followed me into the bathroom. I didn't know he was behind me until I was in the stall and when I turned to close the door he was standing right there and we just started kissing," she drew the quilt up to her chest, "he was afraid that someone would come in so we had to be very quiet. He bolted the stall door and then I lifted up my dress. He sat on the toilet seat and I sat on his lap facing him. It didn't hurt that much." Bill looked at her closely, "So, did you enjoy it?" "It was really awkward," she shrugged, "I mean he was so big and that was pretty scary." "Did he wear a condom?" "No," shaking her head, "it didn't matter anyway because it was before I had my period…Are you upset with me?" Bill frowned, "No, I'm not," and then asked, "is this true?" She wondered why he would ask her that, "Of course it's true." "What happened next?" She looked over at Walter and discovered he was asleep on the rug. "I was pretty scared at first, but I really wanted to, I guess," she realized that their time together was almost over, "he left the bathroom just before the bride walked in with her friends to smoke a joint. I had to sit on the toilet seat with my legs up so they wouldn't notice me." Bill's voice had a weird urgency, "Did you ever see him again?" that she had never heard. "No," shaking her head, "I found out he was married right after that. He introduced me to his wife when I asked him to dance with me again." Bill nodded purposefully. "You're not upset with me are you?" "I'm really surprised," his tone became familiar, "that you would give yourself to a stranger so quickly." "That's why I've never told anyone," with a wary look, "so don't judge me." He crossed his arms over his chest, "Most people would call that rape." "I just told you that I wanted to." "I understand that Sarah, but he abused you, now do *you* understand that?" She didn't want the night to end with an argument but here it was, "Isn't that what most men do?" He clenched his jaw, "I don't think so." "They lie to get what they want and then they leave," she swung her legs off the bed, "unless a girl is stupid enough to believe all the bullshit she is being fed," placed her bare feet on the cold wood floor, "I mean, come on," and took her bra from the chair, "it's almost always just like rape." He watched her fasten the clasp, "All the same, I'm surprised you would lower yourself like that." "I don't want to fight with you," Sarah dressed quickly, "listen," then stood over the daybed, "I have to go," and looked down at Bill before kissing him on the cheek. "I'll see you in class." She nodded and turned away. He watched as she walked to the door and quietly let herself out. Her footfalls made their way through the snow as the candle burned out.

Wednesday, December 25, 1996

Steven stood in the doorway wearing a new pair of dark green corduroy pants. "Why are you sucking in your stomach like that?" Sarah asked. "The length is fine," he took another deep breath, "they're just a little snug," forced his right thumb beneath the waistband and exhaled, "in the waist department." The multicolored lights adorning the tree cast a warm glow over the room. Scraps of blue, red, white, and green wrapping paper were strewn about the beige carpet. Sarah frowned, "I'll exchange them for you tomorrow." The room smelled of pine, wood smoke, and new clothes. "No, that's okay," he shuffled toward the couch, "I can take care of it." A violin sonata was quietly playing on the stereo as snow fell outside the bay windows. The logs in the fireplace crackled. "In that color?" Holly branches were arranged around four thick white candles burning atop the red brick mantel. "You don't have to," he stood in front of the couch, "I'll go sometime next week." Kate was sitting next to Sarah, "We're going to the mall tomorrow anyway," in pink flannel pajamas, "so we can do it for you then," and a new pair of fuzzy pink slippers. He grinned, "That money is already burning a hole in your pocket." Sarah's legs were doubled beneath her, "Do you like that color, honey?" He nodded, "The color is fine." Her dark blue satin robe was drawn over her pale chest, "Didn't the same thing happen last Christmas?" Shaking his head, "It was the year before." She looked up from his waist, "I'm sure they have them in a…" and noted his expression, "that's a thirty-four waist?" "It's just a *little* too snug," he undid the button, "unless I wear them like this." "I'm sure they have them in a thirty-six," she looked away, "unless you want to try a thirty-eight." Kate giggled, "You're getting too fat, dad." "Your father isn't fat," Sarah turned to her, "how would you like it if someone said that about you?" "That wouldn't bother me," Kate shrugged, "because I know it isn't true." "Fat is a pretty," he slapped his stomach with his palms, "a pretty blunt way of putting it," then looked down at them, "don't you think?" Kate turned to her mother, "you should have bought him those pants with an elastic waistband, like the kind grandma wears." He frowned, "You two are so cruel to me sometimes." Sarah looked up at him and smiled, "What about these shirts?" "I really like them." She cleared her throat, "Don't you think that you should try them on?" Kate sat up, "Mr. Pierre Cardin," and patted her father's stomach, "Mrs. Claus must really love her Santa." He picked up the shirts and sat down on the couch between them. "But they're all," he looked through the black and white tags attached to the shirts, "they're all the same size. I haven't grown breasts you know, I've just put on a few inches in the pants department." Kate walked to the fireplace and sat down on the hearth with her back to the fire. "They aren't all the same color are they," Sarah asked before placing her left arm along the back of the couch, "you behave just like a little boy," and ran her fingers through his thick brown hair, "when it comes to trying on clothes." "As opposed to what…a model?"

"How about an adult for a change?" He waved her suggestion away, "I've got the day off." Kate watched her parents on the couch, "You need to be anorexic if you want to be a model," relieved by how happy they seemed. "How about those plus-size models," Sarah suggested, "he could be one of those Mr. Big and Tall models." Kate wondered why they couldn't act this way more often. "Okay," he leaned back, "okay…I can take a hint and starting tomorrow I'll start exercising again." Christmas was one of the few days of the year when it seemed like they truly enjoyed each other. "I'll start jogging again and do a hundred sit-ups every night before bed." Kate wondered what it was about the holidays that always depressed her. "Perhaps you should start with twenty-five," Sarah placed her left hand on his shoulder, "you were so handsome when we were in school," and noted the flesh that had accumulated along his jaw, "I was so jealous of all your girlfriends." He made a face, "You didn't even know I existed until I mustered up the courage to ask you out." "I did," she kissed him on the cheek, "but I was playing it cool." "Come on dad," Kate forced herself to smile, "let's have a fashion show." He rested his elbows on his knees, "Before or after you shovel the driveway?" "I love it when it snows on Christmas," Sarah turned and watched the falling snow, "it's just perfect." "Andrew is coming over later," Kate fingered a button on her pajama top, "I'm sure he'll give you a hand."

The five family portraits on the windowsill had been taken in four-year intervals, starting with the year of Kate's birth. Sarah and Steven had been dating for six months when they discovered she was pregnant. Kate was born in January of '80. Sarah dropped out of SUNY Binghampton after the first semester of her junior year to take care of her little Capricorn. Steven waited tables to support them while he continued school. In the spring of '82, he graduated with a business degree. They were both twenty-two when they married in a small civil ceremony that July. Steven took a job as a regional sales rep in a Utica-based paper company three months later. Sarah became a receptionist in a dental office when Kate started elementary school. She often thought of returning to college and getting a degree but couldn't decide what she wanted to study. Steven was now a national sales manager, and they had recently paid off their house.

He placed the shirts on a large burgundy pillow, "I should have gotten you a snow-blower." "You mean you didn't," Kate pouted, "that's really what I wanted this year." He grinned while suggesting, "You would've been the first girl on the block with one." Sarah took her blue coffee mug off the side table, "I'm surprised Andrew isn't here already," and took a sip of hot chocolate. Kate stretched her arms above her head, "Andrew is spending the morning with his mom," and yawned. "Is his father coming over for dinner as well?" She placed the mug on the table and noticed an important gift. "No," Kate shook her head, "his dad is in Florida." "So it's the three of us," Sarah took the gift off the table, "Andrew and mom," stood up, "sweetheart," crossed to the hearth and sat next to Kate, "you haven't opened all of your presents yet." "Oh, let me guess," she took the gift from her mother and said, "another book," before tearing off the green and red cartoon reindeer wrapping paper. "It's not just any book." Kate looked up, "*Alice in Wonderland*," then at the cover, "that movie gave me nightmares when I was a kid," before thumbing through the pages. Tenniel's illustration of Alice swimming with a mouse in a pool of tears drew her attention to the text beneath it, *"Perhaps it doesn't understand English," thought Alice. "I daresay it's a French mouse, come over with William the Conqueror. (For, with all her knowledge of history, Alice had no very clear notion how long ago anything happened.) So she began again: "Où est ma chatte?" which was the first sentence in her French lesson book. The mouse gave a sudden leap out of the water, and seemed to quiver with fright.* "It was practically my guide to life when I was sixteen and I hope you enjoy it as much as I did." "But it's a *children's* book." "You'll find a lot of really beautiful poems hidden in the stories," she smiled, "the more you read into it the more rewarding it becomes... it's a very complex book." Kate kissed her dutifully on the cheek, "Thanks," and swallowed her frustration, "but you know I'm not a little girl anymore." "I know that sweetheart and by giving you this...I wasn't," Sarah looked closely at her daughter, "I really love the person you are...we both really love the person you are, and the young woman you're becoming, and we are so proud of you." Kate shook her head, "Oh, mom." Sarah watched as she began to blush, "I just thought it might give you some perspective as to what sort of people your parents were, before we became your parents." Steven handed Kate another gift, "It looks like this is for you too." She looked up while taking it out of his hand, "This must be from you." He grinned, "Really?" She nodded, "I can tell by the way it's wrapped." "Remember Kate," he watched her rip the green paper off the book, "you can't judge a gift by its wrapping." "Or a book by its cover," Sarah placed her left arm around Kate's shoulder, "that's from both of us."

Thursday, January 20, 1977

Robert pulled off the black and yellow wool hat, "So you haven't seen her since Christmas?" Brian ran his fingers through his blond beard then yawned, "You finally got a haircut." Robert glanced at the couch, a thick green blanket covered the brown cushions, and a pillow was tucked beneath the armrest—and assumed Brian had been taking a nap.

Robert sat behind the wheel of the '68 Falcon with the engine running. He turned the heater up and clapped his gloved hands as cold air blew out of the vents. The car was warming up in the empty parking lot. The dark sky was overcast, another heavy snow was looming.

"Yeah, well," he nodded, "I didn't have much say in the matter." The living room was warm and well lit. Molly, a German Shepherd with severe arthritis, slowly raised her head off her makeshift bed and tentatively wagged her tail. "It's about time you did that," monthly disability checks from the VA subsidized the meager income Brian scraped together as a carpenter, "though it doesn't make sense to cut that much off in the middle of winter." Robert stuffed the wool hat into the right front pocket of his overcoat and looked at him expectantly, "Not since Christmas?"

Robert turned on the headlights. The snow banks bordering the parking lot were blackened with car exhaust. He'd opened the store at eight in the morning; the day had been dull and uneventful.

A log crackled in the iron stove and sent sparks onto the large slab of bluestone. A bronze Marine plaque hung on the wall to the left of the window. "That's right," Brian turned and walked to the stove as the log began to hiss, "I guess you heard about that fire down in Philmont last week," he'd joined the Marines with two friends, "in that textile factory," the day after they'd graduated from high school. Robert pulled off the leather gloves with fingers still numb from the cold. "You must have heard about that." He stuffed them into the left front pocket of his overcoat, "Have you spoken to her?"

He put his right foot on the brake and shifted the car into reverse. He put his left hand on the steering wheel, stretched his right arm across the top of the front seat, and looked over his shoulder. He took his foot off the brake and the car began moving backwards as he slowly turned the steering wheel to the left.

Robert walked toward Molly's bed, and she eyed him as he knelt down. "Hey, girl," he rubbed the warm dark brown fur between her ears and whispered, "why do you look so sad?" Brian said, "Two five-hundred gallon propane tanks went up," over his shoulder as he crouched before the stove. Her tail beat an uneven rhythm

64

against the mattress. Floor to ceiling bookshelves covered the wall opposite the couch. The shelves were filled with rows of secondhand books. An eight-track stereo, a turntable, and two large speakers were also installed on the shelves. The rows of albums beneath the stereo consisted mostly of blues, some folk, and rock-n-roll.

He shifted the car into drive, turned the steering wheel in the direction of the exit, and placed his foot on the gas. The snow tires crushed chunks of mud-colored ice. The car slid to a slow stop as exhaust billowed out of the muffler.

A portable black and white television set was situated on a lower shelf—a scene from Jimmy Carter's inauguration ceremony on the silent screen. Brian fed another log into the stove, "and the explosion took out two blocks of buildings. That's like dropping two thousand pound bombs right on their mark." Robert began massaging the back of Molly's neck. Brian's left hand had been blown off by a grenade in the battle to take Hue City in February of '68. His two friends had died during the siege of Khe Sanh a month later and were buried a few miles away from their high school. Robert stood up and unbuttoned his overcoat, "Have you spoken to her?" The black buttons were still cold to the touch.

He looked to his left and watched the approaching station wagon. The headlights fell upon the dark wood paneling as it passed. He eased his foot off the brake, turned the wheel to the right, and the car moved onto the slush-covered road.

There was a large color map of the world on the wall above the couch. "No I haven't," Brian closed the stove, "but she'll call every once in a while to see if I'm still alive," stood up slowly, "or when she needs something," and turned around, "just like everyone else." Robert tugged at the wool scarf around his neck, "Like every month or so?" He nodded, "About that," and with a smile added, "you know that haircut makes you look like Donny Osmond." He looked down at Molly, "Thanks, that's the look I'm going for." She barked twice, and Brian laughed, "Maybe more like Marie," then nodded at the couch, "so are you just going to stand there feeling sorry for yourself or do you want to sit down and do that?" Brian's beard covered most of the scars on his neck and the left side of his face. He removed his coat and draped it over the armrest before sitting down on the edge of the couch, "Do you think she's dating anyone?" then eyed the plastic bag of marijuana on the coffee table. "Maybe . . .but if she was, I'd be the last person to hear about it." "You met me," Robert looked over at him, "when we were going out." Brian nodded and said, "Only because you get high," with a shrug.

He stepped on the gas while thinking of the conversation he'd had with Brian over the phone. The car accelerated as he drove out of town.

Sarah had dumped him five months ago without an explanation, "The guy could have called when you were over there," and it still really hurt. The other day Robert told his younger sister that it felt like a family of rats had burrowed into his chest. "Or she's got his picture on her bedroom wall?" Brian cleared his throat, "Why don't you just ask her?" Robert shrugged, "She won't tell me and the last time I called," then muttered something under his breath. "What?" He shook his head and frowned, "never mind."

A speeding rig hauling an empty flatbed sent a thick spray of slush over the windshield. The wipers pulled and pressed the oncoming headlights across the windshield.

"Never mind what," Brian sat on the opposite end of the couch, "Perry Mason?" and adjusted the pillow behind his back. There was a packet of rolling papers on the coffee table. "So do you think the guy who fired the blank at Gilmore's execution knew he didn't have a real bullet in his gun?" There was a book to the right of the papers with a torn dust jacket, **"A great book that has no peer among narratives of its kind"** in red letters above a paragraph in black letters, **"Great commanders have mostly been dull writers. Rommel was a born writer as well as a born fighter. The impact that he made on the world with the sword will be deepened by his power with the pen. No commander in history has written an account of his campaigns to match the vividness and value of Rommel's. No other commander has proven such a graphic picture of his operations and methods of command"** From the introduction by Capt. Liddle Hart Beneath the quotation, there was a black and white photograph of the North Africa desert with tank tracks criss-crossing the sand. "Probably not, but what does that have to do with my sister?" A stainless steel Zippo engraved with the USMC emblem. "Is a blank going to have the same kind of kick?" A mortar shell casing fashioned into an ashtray filled with cigarette butts. "The rifles they used don't kick all that much." A half-empty quart of Jack Daniel's was next to the ashtray. "They send you in there to do a job…and you aim for the heart…you're there to hit a target." A shot glass with a drop of amber bourbon was beside the bottle. Robert turned to him, "Their target." Brian shook his head, "As far as I'm concerned he wanted to die. He was just as fed up by the circus as the rest of us."

Robert glanced at the speedometer, realized the car was going too fast, and let up on the gas. The white needle slowly fell as the car passed a snow-covered field.

Robert leaned back on the couch and eyed the bag of what looked like a half ounce of homegrown, "You think so?" He had twenty dollars in his wallet, "I mean that just seems so extreme," two folded tens that he'd taken from the cash register. Brian removed the pipe from the breast pocket of his denim shirt, "the only people who *really* didn't want him to die," leaned forward, and placed it on the coffee table between them, "were the ones selling newspapers," Brian had carved the pipe, "and I think they should have shown the fucking thing on television," from a branch pruned off the cherry tree in his backyard. Robert studied the flickering image of the White House while asking, "To stop people from killing by showing someone being executed on television?" He reached forward, unrolled the bag, and removed a small bud. "No, so the taxpayers could see that," Brian pointed at himself with the end of his left arm, "could see that they were getting their money's worth and I'm not saying that I would have watched it though…I've seen enough people die." Robert shrugged, "So why even bother with the blank?" Brian frowned, "Peace of mind." The bud between his thumb and forefinger, "That sounds pretty half-assed to me," was moist and smelled faintly of the meadow it had been grown in. "Would you want that on your head?" Robert took the pipe off the coffee table, "Did you have blanks for your M16?" "Hell, no." He packed the bud into the bowl with his thumb, "Right so—" "I was trying to stop the Viet Cong from killing me and the men in my company." "Right so," he took the Zippo off the table, "they execute people to keep others from killing," and placed the stem of the pipe between his lips. Brian said, "I wasn't shooting people in the back at gas stations." He flipped the cover on the Zippo and flicked the wheel with his thumb. The blackened wick sparked as it ignited. Robert said, "They should have given Calley's company blanks," before holding the yellow flame over the bowl. "They should have never sent him to Vietnam in the first place." It dipped into the bowl and ignited the marijuana as Robert drew deeply on the pipe. "But shit, man, that's the candy-ass army for you. They don't even train you properly...bunch of draftees with no fucking clue. Calley couldn't even read a goddamn map." He snapped the Zippo shut, removed the pipe from his mouth and exhaled with a practiced nonchalance. The pipe was smoking from both ends and his mouth tasted of lighter fluid. He offered it to Brian. "Naw, I'm okay." A bluish cloud hung over Robert's head while he took another long hit. The logs in the stove crackled and popped. He turned to Brian and smiled before exhaling, "I don't know how you do it." Brian looked at Robert, "I just put the seeds in the ground," then pulled at his beard, "it isn't rocket science," with his right hand.

Robert remembered the intersection and slowly stepped on the brake while turning the wheel to the right. The headlights cut across a snow covered pasture and a frozen pond. He was a half-mile from Brian's house.

"Yeah, but," Robert's smile grew into an ear to ear grin, "but two hits and I'm nice and stoned," the room softened around him, "you sure you don't want any," as he sank back into the couch. "No, I'm okay, that's yours." He thought of the cherry tree in the backyard and the birds on its branches when they were filled with fruit late last July. He'd driven over with Sarah, and they'd surprised Brian in the workshop where he was refurbishing a couch. They'd hung out with him that afternoon, drinking red wine from a gallon jug and smoking his homegrown. A group of blue jays had swooped down on the robins picking at the cherries beneath the tree. Before the afternoon was over, Brian had set up the barbecue and grilled some hamburgers. The tomatoes in his garden had been a bit under ripe but tasted fine with a pinch of salt. They'd eaten off of paper plates at the picnic table as the jays had continued their noisy occupation of the cherry tree. Robert sighed as he leaned forward and placed the pipe on the coffee table. Brian was watching the muted television. "So the last time I called her...she told me never to call again." "That's pathetic." Nodding his head, "Exactly, you'd think she'd have a little common courtesy. A little—" "No man, you're pathetic." Robert recoiled, "No, I'm not," and gave him a wounded look. "You're like a little lovesick puppy dog."

The car pulled into the recently plowed driveway and made its way up the steep incline. Brian heard the car in the driveway and finished reading the paragraph *A large concentration of enemy troops in the Bois de Riencourt was destroyed by the fire of the Panzer Regiment's tanks as they drove past. Over to the left, a giant pillar of smoke belched up from a burning enemy petrol tanker and numerous saddled horses stampeded rider-less across the plain. Then heavy enemy artillery fire from the southwest crashed into the division, but was made unable to halt its attack. Over a broad front and in great depth, tanks, anti-aircraft guns, field guns all with infantry mounted on them, raced across country east of the road. Vast clouds of dust rose high in the evening sky over the flat plain.* He closed the book and placed it on the coffee table. The car door slammed as he stood up.

"It's not like that," Robert shook his head, "I can't even sleep most nights. All I do is think about her." "You need to beat-off more often…that's what works for me when I can't sleep." "Thanks," Robert realized that he must have said something wrong, "thanks for sharing," and that he should pay for the grass and leave immediately, "I really appreciate that." "Anytime." The thought of driving home without knowing why Sarah didn't even want to speak to him anymore filled him with dread, "So, when was the last time she called you?" "Man," Brian shook his head, "you've got it bad." "So," Robert reached in his back pocket and pulled out his wallet, "like that's a crime…or something," took out the tens, "but seeing as how you're her brother, you've obviously got a lot more in common with her than I do." "Christ, when I was your age." Robert tossed the folded bills on the table. "I had a lot more important things to worry about than a piece of ass," Brian looked at the money, "but you are reminding me of the time a girl‑ ‑" "She isn't a piece of ass," he scowled while standing up, "but I guess you've got a lot more important things to worry about anyway." "Sorry, pal," Brian had lived alone for five years, "you aren't the only one who's ever had his heart broken." Robert didn't want to sit down again, "What happened to you?" afraid that would make him look even more confused than he already felt. "It's a long story." He shrugged, "I'm not in any hurry," before sitting on the edge of the couch, "so what happened to you?" On television, the American flag was waving above Arlington cemetery. Brian exhaled slowly through his nose, "I'm sorry my sister has made you feel this way. And I know you don't want to be hearing this right now but—" "Do you think you could just call her and just talk to her?" Brian stood up and walked to the pile of wood stacked on the floor next to the stove, "I can't do that." He watched Brian take a log off the pile, "Why not?" "Just listen to me," he turned around with the log in his hand. "I mean, all you have to do is call her—" "Just relax, man—" "I don't think," Robert crossed his arms over his chest, "that's too much to ask." Molly barked twice as she struggled to get up. "I want you to hear me out," Brian knelt in front of the stove, "after that, if you think it's still a good idea…I might do it." Molly slowly made her way over to Robert while dragging her rear legs. "Yeah, okay." She placed her pointed nose over his left knee. "That sounds fair," Robert ran his right hand through the thick fur behind her ears. "I'm just going to ask you one question," Brian lay the log on the fire, "Okay?" "Yeah," Robert continued rubbing her head, "yeah, okay." "How are you going to," Brian stood up, "force someone to do something they don't want to do?" He leaned back on the couch, "I don't understand." "That part is obvious," Brian laughed. "Why don't you explain it then…instead of trying to make me feel like an idiot." He shook his head, "She must have a reason for not wanting to speak to you anymore," then sighed before asking, "and you know what?" Robert shrugged, "No, what?" "It probably doesn't have anything to do with you." "How do you know that?" "Because if it did, she would have told you." "But I just," he swallowed hard, "I still love her." "Well, she doesn't feel the same way about you." Robert looked down at Molly, who had positioned herself between his knees. "And you can't take that personally." He frowned, "How can I not take it personally?" Brian turned off the television, "Because that's her decision and it doesn't have anything to do with you," and began thumbing through a long row of albums. "I must have done something wrong…I really don't know what it was and that is driving me crazy." Brian turned to Robert while holding out his copy of *Highway 61 Revisited* and asked, "Do you like Dylan?"

Wednesday, July 16, 1997

Kate imagined a camera filming their expressions as she approached him. Andrew was wearing his Burger King uniform and a pair of black converse high-tops. Kate's summer dress had been borrowed from the theater's wardrobe department. Andrew's name-tag was pinned above the pocket on his shirt. He stepped around the bench and stood in the center of the sidewalk. She leaned into his lanky frame as they kissed. "Why don't we walk to your house?" She rested her head on his shoulder and kissed him on the neck, "Alright." His uniform smelled of French fry grease, "It's not as hot today." She looked closely at his eyes as they began walking hand in hand. "Don't you have work?" He swallowed dryly, "I told you that I gave notice." "That isn't," she turned to him, "for another two weeks," why did he seem so sullen, "Andrew?"

He saw himself standing behind the counter fingering the buttons on the cash register, "I really don't feel like going in today," reciting orders into a microphone, "or any other day," handing over warm bags of fast food, "fuck that," and counting out change for the next eight hours.

She squeezed his right hand, "If you don't go, they'll fire you." He shrugged, "Let them," as a grin pushed at his mouth, "the only good thing about the job is the uniform." They walked past the daycare center—the lawn was filled with dandelions and children's toys. "Maybe you should just keep it," she suggested. He realized he would be broke again, "Yeah?" She nodded with a smile. A dark blue sedan with tinted windows raced past them. "You think so?" She pinched his ass, "You know I like how tight those pants are." He exclaimed, "That's because you're a pervert," while removing a cardboard crown from his back pocket and placing it atop his bleached blond head. "That's because you're a very good teacher," she linked her right arm through his left, "Do you think they'll make you pay for it?" He thought for a moment before saying, "It's probably worth more than my last paycheck," then added, "I'm going to wear it to school everyday." She kissed him on the cheek, "so you *are* in a good mood." "It feels great," he hunched his shoulders, "to quit something you hate." She watched a green and white UTA bus come to a stop across the street, "How did it go with your mom last night?" He followed her eyes, "Are you sure you want to walk?" "Yeah," she nodded, "it makes the time we have together last longer." The deep blue sky was almost cloudless. He watched an elderly woman bent over a cane slowly moving away from the bus. The shadows from oaks lining the sidewalk were cast on the lawns of the houses facing the street. "I'd like to spend the night," he turned to her, "if that's okay with you." "I got my period this morning." The bus slowly pulled away from the curb leaving a haze of diesel fumes behind. "You know that doesn't bother me." The UTA logo on the rear of the bus *We're here to get you there* was coated with a grainy film of black exhaust. A sprinkler sent a thick stream of water over a bed of roses and onto the sidewalk. She smiled, "It's nice and cold," and wiped the drops off her face. He thought about the argument he'd had with his mother the night before, "Wouldn't it be cool if you could spend your entire life reading every single book in the library?" The lawns smelled of roses and cut grass. "Including all the books in foreign languages?" Sunlight was reflected in the windows and on the hoods of the passing cars. "Sure, but you'd have to teach yourself every major language to do it and you could only learn those languages from the books available in the library." "Yeah, but," she removed a pair of mirrored sunglasses from her purse and put them on, "you can't really learn another language just from reading books." They walked by two young black girls flinging an orange Frisbee back and forth. "Those books are there because people who speak those languages go to the library, right?" She nodded. "So it wouldn't be all that difficult to find people to help you." The Frisbee sailed over a row of shrubs. He speculated, "maybe they would do it in exchange for improving their English," then spoke to his reflection, "those make you look like a cop," in her sunglasses. She stuck out her tongue before asking, "How would you support yourself?" A catbird called from a nearby tree. He thought for a moment as they continued walking, "work nights at some shitty part-time job to pay the bills," then realized he was about to be fired from the job he was describing, "or teaching English," he clasped his hands together and cracked his knuckles, "someone checked out that copy of your uncle's Vietnam book." She noticed the Burger King on the opposite side of the street and frowned, "Oh, really." He jammed his hands in his front pockets, "I was looking for it before," as the traffic moved through the intersection, "while I was waiting for you and it wasn't on the shelf." She cleared her throat, "Are you sure you want to do this?" He was toying with the idea of treating her to some French fries and a chocolate shake, "Definitely." They would sit in a booth and

continue their conversation—just like two normal human beings—and when they finished their snack they would stand up
and walk out. "What about that car?" The signal changed, "I would
have spent every penny I made," as he realized he didn't have
enough money to treat her, "just to keep it running." They crossed
the street as she asked, "What about California?" "We wouldn't
have gotten it out of my neighborhood…Maybe your mom will
loan us her car?" They stepped over the curb in unison. "Yeah
right," she squeezed his hand, "to drive across the country," as
they walked by the Burger King, "not in a million years…I still
want to go after we graduate." He was quick to suggest, "Why
don't we just take the bus?" "You obviously don't want to do this
as badly as I do." "Oh, you think just because," he let go of her
hand and stopped walking, "I quit my shitty job that I don't want
to go." "I didn't say that." "Well you made it sound that way," he
felt ridiculous, "I'll get *another* shitty job I promise," watching his
angry reflection in her cheap sunglasses, "*and* a car by next summer,"
as he placed his hands on his waist. She looked down at the scuffed
tips of his sneakers, "Are you sure?" He didn't want to argue with
her, "Sure I'm sure," and didn't want her to be angry with him,
"Do you know how many dead Versaces it takes to screw in a
lightbulb?" She punched him on the shoulder, "You shouldn't
make jokes about that…it's just so sad." "Who cares?" "How can
you say that?" "People get shot everyday," he hawked up the phlegm
in his throat and spat on the sidewalk, "murdered in cold blood,"
then made a gun with his right hand, "but when it happens to
some celebrity," he pointed his gun at a passing pick-up and, "pow,"
pulled the trigger. "And what about all those other people he
supposedly killed?" Kate asked. "Exactly and that's my point, you
didn't hear about them with round-the-clock news coverage and
maybe if you had he would have been caught…like months ago."

She frowned, "You're only making jokes about this because his name is Andrew." He shook his head, "You know that I'm right." Dozen of sparrows hopped around the large puddle beside the fire hydrant. "Regardless, you shouldn't make jokes about it." They splashed themselves while singing in the gutter. "So how did it go with your mom last night?" "What made you think of that," he smirked, "male prostitutes?" She stopped walking, "Can't you be serious for a minute?" He took off the cardboard crown, "It didn't go very well," folded it up, "he's going to move in next month," and slid it into his back pocket, "and I can't do anything about it." She took a step back, "That is just so unfair." "Nothing in life is fair, Kate. And I really hate it when you say shit like that. You sound so naïve." They began walking as Kate exclaimed, "She doesn't care about anyone other than herself." Andrew wondered if becoming an adult meant that most of the adults he already knew would no longer seem like assholes, or that he would simply become an asshole as well. "So I told her I wanted," he cleared his throat, "to live with my dad." "And what," she removed her sunglasses and put them back in her purse, "sleep on the couch in his living room?" Andrew sighed, "I could just get my own place," even if it meant holding down a full-time job while going through his senior year, "that might be my only escape." Her eyes widened, "You could live with us," as she clutched his arms, "you know my parents won't care…please." He furrowed his brow, "Of course they would." She drew herself closer to him, "They really, really like you." "No," he stepped away, "no way." She began to pout, "Why not?" A white plastic shopping bag was twisted around the tree branch above her head. "I already spend way too much time over at your house as it is." "I'm sure if we talked to them about it." He said, "No," before turning away from her. She yanked at his sleeve, "You know they think of you as family." He turned around, "I don't need their charity." She withdrew her hand, "That's not what this is." "Well," he folded his arms across his stomach, "what would you call it?" She frowned, "You are so unbelievably pigheaded sometimes," and they walked up the block in silence.

Friday, November 12, 1976

Bill was thumbing through the *Observer Dispatch* while sitting on the red brick hearth before the fireplace. "There's a little wine left," Mary called from the kitchen, "are you sure you don't want any?" as she placed the last few forks and knives in the dishwasher. He looked up, "No, that's okay," before reading the plot synopsis for an episode of *Sanford and Son. The Committeeman—The premise of the script helps the cornball series tonight.* "What?" *Fred Sanford, believe it or not, is picked by the mayor to represent Watts on a community relations board* Closing the dishwasher door she yelled, "Do you want any more wine?" *and has a grand time bugging his peers.* Bill looked up and said, "I'm fine," in a louder voice *Guest Edward Andrews appears playing one of his specialties* and added, "you go ahead." *–the slick businessman—an idiot, in this case, who offers Sanford a bribe.* After drying her hands on a blue dishtowel and letting down her long brown hair, she entered the living room, "What are you doing?" *Red Foxx, Pro Edwards, and comic Ronnie Schell amuse themselves in this one.* Bill looked up as she walked toward him, "I'm warming up the television," and crumpled up the newspaper in his hands. She was wearing a brown cashmere cardigan, a black turtleneck, a beige wool skirt that fell just below her knees, black pumps, and a pair of black stockings. He turned and stuffed the newspaper beneath the andiron. "You're what?" Her bemused tone annoyed him. Bill stood up and took the blue and red cardboard box of matches off the mantle, "Is there any brandy left?" "Sure," she nodded, "I bought a new bottle today." He knelt before the fireplace while extracting a wooden match, "May I have a glass?" and struck it on the side of the box. She took a half-step toward him, "What about the wine?" He held the match to the newspapers, "Save it for tomorrow," and as the text ignited, he moved the flame from one crumpled fold to the next, "I don't want anymore." She continued watching, "I might as well finish it now," the paper catch fire, "because it won't taste as good tomorrow." When the flame swayed too close to his fingers, "There you go," he tossed the match into the fire. "That's the last of the good Bordeaux," she was fed up with looking at the back of his head, "you know." He shrugged, "I'm sure we'll be able to find some more."

The framed color photograph on the wooden mantel had been taken in Paris during their honeymoon in June of '73. Bill asked a passerby to photograph them as they stood on the steps of Sacré-Coeur. She is kissing him on the cheek as he smiles into the living room. They spent three happy weeks in Paris.

She stood behind him, "What would you like to listen to?" hoping he would ask her to put on a symphony. He rested his hands on the knees, "It's up to you," of his dark green corduroy pants. "Something that goes well with the snow," Mary ventured, "or something more romantic?" He muttered, "if you'd like," and blew on the flames slowly spreading through the newspaper, "the wine was really good with the roast." "You don't think it was a bit overdone?" He turned around, "Maybe a bit." She placed her hands on her hips, "I didn't ruin it though?" Bill looked back at the expanding flames, "Not at all," as they caught on the twigs. She shook her head, "I shouldn't have left it on the stove," took three steps forward and sat next to him. "Your potatoes were great." The fire reflected in his eyes. He was wearing the wool sweater she had woven for him the winter before they married. She looked at him closely, "Oh," and smiled. "It was a very good meal." "Well," she rested her hands on the edge of the hearth, "you always love my scalloped potatoes," the amber pendant she wore around her neck on a thin gold chain swayed in front of her chest, "You aren't getting tired of them?" He shook his head, "Not at all," and blew on the growing fire. He removed a narrow log from the stack of red oak and carefully placed it atop the burning kindling. "Are you alright, Bill?" "Why do you ask?" She made a gesture with her right hand, "Well," and quickly clasped it in her left hand, "because," as if she had just snatched a moth. He pretended not to notice, "Why?" "You just seem a bit strange," she pressed her hands in her lap, "maybe a bit distant." He nodded, "I was just fine until you asked." "Oh, come on," she looked away, "we're supposed to be having a nice evening together." He added another log to the crackling fire. "I've hardly seen you all week," she complained. He looked at her closely, "Do you think I could have that glass of brandy now?" She placed her hands on the hearth and stood up, "I think I'll have one as well," then walked to the kitchen.

The flames wove their way through the wood. The door swung closed behind her as she crossed to the counter. She took the bottle of Bordeaux and poured the remainder of it into a stained wine glass. He held his hands in front of the fire, spread his fingers apart and warm air enveloped them. A thin trail of red wine ran down the neck of the bottle and streaked across the white label as she drained the glass in one swallow. The fire crackled and a few sparks landed in front of his knees. She crossed to the cabinets above the toaster-oven and took two snifters off the shelf and placed them on the counter. He watched the sparks fade. She walked to the pantry—the brandy was on the shelf next to the gin and dry vermouth. He thought about Sarah while staring at the flames. She tore the mail-in-rebate off the neck of the bottle and unscrewed the metal cap. She poured even amounts of amber brandy into the glasses. He pulled the metal screen across the fireplace and turned around as she entered the living room.

She managed a smile while handing him the snifter. He swirled the brandy around in slow circles before holding it beneath his nose. She sat on the couch, "The new bottle came with a rebate," and crossed her right leg over her left knee. He shrugged before taking a sip. She looked out the window, "it's really coming down outside," and watched the falling snow. He swallowed before saying, "Tonight through tomorrow afternoon." She looked away from the window, "come here, sweetheart," and smiled as he stood up and crossed to the couch. She placed her arm around his shoulder, "your back is so warm," and then they kissed. "You've got a bit of chocolate here," she carefully scraped the frosting off his lower lip with her thumbnail. The logs shifted in the fire. He leaned back on the cushion, "What did you want to listen to?" She swung her feet onto his lap, "This is just fine." He pulled off her black pumps, "You've been waiting to do this all day," and dropped them on the carpet. She wiggled her stockinged feet, "This feels so nice," and as he took them in his hands she asked, "How many weeks has it been since we have had any time together?" He nodded, "Work has been so hectic lately," while tracing a line along the arch of her left foot. She sighed, "Are you feeling better?" as the amber caught the lamplight. "Yes." She reached behind her head with her right hand and took the snifter off the side table, "What was the matter?" She sipped the brandy and when he didn't respond she tried again, "Are you just tired?" He nodded thoughtfully while watching the burning logs, "Feels like I'm getting a second wind though." She smiled, "That's good because we still have a few items left on tonight's agenda." "That's right," the low-cut black nightgown, "I'm getting a fashion show as well," that she had taken from a shopping bag and promised to model for him later in the bedroom. She pressed his right hand between the arches of her feet, "Unless you're too tired." He removed his hand, "No, not at all," and rubbed his nose. She tilted her head and watched the falling snow. His fingers smelled faintly of shoe leather. A gust of wind pressed the snow against the window. "Have you seen Walter?" "Not since I fed him," her eyes remained on the window, "he's probably sleeping in your study…you really need to trim his nails." "I'll do that this weekend." "Promise?" He nodded, "I'll do it tomorrow." "I caught him scratching up the duvet this afternoon." He took another sip of brandy before saying, "So tell me more about your day." "There is something that I want to," she crossed her ankles in his lap, "that I need to tell you," and cleared her throat, "Nancy called this morning and—" "How are they doing?" "She thinks Dan is having an affair." "Really?" She quickly added, "You can't tell him any of this." He looked at her skeptically, "That's absurd, Mary." Nancy and Dan were two of their closest friends. "Why would you say that?" Mary and Nancy had been inseparable when they were teenagers and attended Syracuse University together. Nancy met Dan in their junior year, and Dan introduced

Mary to his close friend Bill. "Because he would have told me about it," Bill then asked, "She's due in February right?" With a nod, "I don't think he would have told you." When Bill had confided in Dan about his relationship with Sarah last spring, he'd become so angry that he'd threatened to tell Mary. "I know more about Dan than I do about you." "Maybe we should both have a talk with her then," Mary suggested, "because she is really upset." "Why does she think he's having an affair?" "He's been very distant and they haven't had sex in months." "Hell Mary, that could be most of the couples we know," he looked away, "we aren't intimate that often anymore…so does that mean I'm having an affair?" She responded quickly, "No, and I didn't mean that," not wanting an old fight to inhabit the warm place they were in, "but I'm not Nancy." He pursed his lips, "Do you think she's just being hysterical…because of the pregnancy?" She nodded, "Why don't I tell her that." He smiled, "Smash a grapefruit in her face and then tell her to," then imitated James Cagney, "to snap out of it, see." She laughed, "We shouldn't be joking about this." He placed both hands on her feet, "Dan is far too uptight," and squeezed her toes for emphasis, "to do something like that." "No, he isn't." "He is way too Catholic an—" "Well, I don't think—" "—And they have a beautiful daughter and another baby on the way." She didn't want to play the skeptic, "What does that have to do with it?" "Everything," shrugging his shoulders, "or nothing at all." "Nancy is even thinking about hiring a detective to follow him around." "Wow," he began laughing, "it's already a real soap opera…why don't you do it instead? You would be saving them money and it would get you out of the house until you go back to work." She encouraged him, "I could get a blond wig and wear your beige raincoat—" "And a big Band-Aid over your nose," he interjected, "just like Jack Nicholson in *Chinatown*." She sipped her brandy while thinking of Faye Dunaway on the run, "That was such a good film," and re-crossed her ankles, "you know last spring when we had them over for dinner?" "Last May," he began caressing her feet, "when you made your spareribs or at Easter?" "It was last May I guess," she nodded, "and Dan got really drunk." "I remember someone else doing that as well. You were so sick the next morning...do you remember that...you thought you were going to die." The lump in her throat had grown cold, "Dan helped me while you and Nancy were out on the patio." He scratched the back of his head, "I vaguely remember this." "Dan insisted that he help me." "I do remember talking to Nancy for awhile...just the two of us on the porch...Why?" With a sigh, "he made a pass at me in the kitchen." Bill said, "Really," while thinking about how he should respond. Mary calculated how much of the truth he needed to know. He considered being graciously blindsided, "wow," or acting jealous, "what happened?" She considered his question, "Dan was telling me how important our friendship was to them and then." Bill decided the safest way to react was to be jealous, "And then what?" Mary realized that a half-truth was better than a blatant lie, "And then he started telling me how attractive I was, how pretty I looked in the skirt I was wearing and then . . .You aren't upset with me are you?" "No," her confession was arousing him, "I'm not." "And then we started kissing." He managed to sound skeptical, "In the kitchen?" "It was quite passionate." She seemed too poised to be telling the truth, "What do you mean by that?" "Well, I mean the way that he was so...really aggressive," she looked away from him, "that we were kissing and then—" "The way you were kissing each other," his bemused smile, "what, on the mouth?" She took another sip of brandy, "It was just very spontaneous, you know? We didn't plan it. He was just...I thought he just wanted to help me with the dishes—" "Why didn't you tell me about this before?" She shrugged, "Because it seemed harmless enough and we were really drunk." He didn't believe her, "Did you think I'd be angry," and he couldn't disguise his doubt, "if you told me?" "No, I didn't," and that pleased her, "but I really didn't want to think about how you'd react," she smiled apologetically, "and make a big deal out of it." He referred to the glass in her hand, "Because you were drunk and—" "And supposedly these things happen," her tone was edged with exasperation, "although it has never happened before and I'm certainly not interested in it happening again." He nodded, "And you think that Dan is?" She pointed at the window, "I mean his wife was sitting right there while he was telling her closest friend how he's always wanted to take her to bed and what we were going to do when we got there." "You didn't tell Mary about this?" "No, no, and I never will and besides it's too late for me to do that. I feel so bad for her though, because he *is* capable of that, of cheating on her." The logs shifted, sending a few sparks through the metal screen. "Well, he hasn't told me anything about it and I really think he would have." Mary wondered if Bill would confront Dan with her muddled confession before saying, "He didn't tell you he made a pass at your wife. So why would he tell you he's having an affair?" The wind pressed on the windows. "Dan was really drunk," adjusting his pants to accommodate his erection, "I doubt he even remembers." "But that doesn't mean he isn't unhappy and he couldn't be having an affair." He realized the dinner party in May, "Is that why people have affairs," happened a few weeks after he told Dan about his relationship with Sarah, "because they're unhappy?" "I think so," she paused, "I mean that's an oversimplification, but, yes, I think it's true." He leaned forward, "They've been married for four years," and placed his elbows on his knees. She took her feet off his lap and tucked them beneath his right leg, "they got married the year before we did." He clasped his fingers together and cracked his knuckles, "They have a two-year-old girl," not knowing what else to say, "with another one on the way." "Well, I'm not in any rush," she fingered the pendant while adding, "in fact, I'd be perfectly happy if we never had kids," which is what he wanted to hear.

He drained the brandy. "Are you happy, Bill?" Examining the smudged prints around the empty glass, "Are you asking me if I'm having an affair?" "Why do you keep bringing this up," her eyes narrowed, "I just want to know if you are happy." "Yes, yes," nodding his head mechanically, "yes, I'm happy." "Would—" "—And no, I wouldn't." She thought of all the nights he spent sleeping in his study, "Sometimes I think you would be happier with someone else." "No, absolutely not, why would you say that?" She held out her glass, "Do you want mine?" "Sure," he noticed her anxious expression while taking her glass, "why do you feel that way?" "You can be so withdrawn sometimes," she placed her feet back on his lap, "a lot of times I feel like I don't know you as well as I used to," and crossed her ankles, "or as well as I thought I did." "You mean," he took a sip, "that I've changed?" Her cheeks were flushed from the alcohol, "No, well, maybe," and her voice carried a soft lilt, "I idealized you a lot more then…before we got married and really started living together." "That conversation with Nancy really bothered you." With a nod, "I probably made it seem more dramatic than it was." "How do you think I would've reacted if you'd told me about it last spring?" and before she could respond, "Did you want to sleep with him?" She looked at him crossly, "No," and wondered if he was serious, "with you two sitting out on the patio?" Glancing down at her toenails encased in the pantyhose, "it's not all that uncommon," that were painted the same blood red as her fingernails. "That's really sad," she gave him a wounded look, "I'm not a faithless person." He noted her glazed eyes, "I was making a generalization," and realized she was very drunk. She crossed her arms over her chest and scowled. "Hey," holding up his hands, "don't get mad at me," in surrender. "Well, don't you go making," she wanted to curse him, "those disgusting insinuations." "Are you drunk?" "No, not at all," she swung her legs off his lap and placed her feet on the carpet. "Why don't you just answer me?" Mary looked intently at the fireplace, "What was your question," and waited for the room to stop shifting in its place, "Bill?" He cleared his throat, "If you thought I was having an affair, would you do the same thing?" "Well," she responded through clenched teeth, "I don't think that you are," and when she swallowed, "we are just trying to have a nice evening together," a bit of bile lingered on the back of her tongue, "just the two of us," she rested her head on his shoulder, "and I don't want to fight with you anymore." Brushing her hair away from his mouth, "I think we've both had too much to drink." She placed her lips against his ear and whispered, "I want you to know that I would never, ever do that to us." He closed his eyes, "I know." She removed her head from his shoulder, "Let's go to bed," stood up and placed her hands around his wrists before pulling him off the couch, "we can talk about it there." He wavered on his feet before they embraced. "You're not *that* drunk, are you?" "No, just a bit jealous, that's probably what my problem is," and smiled into her face, "let's see what your new nightgown looks like."

Friday, December 19, 1997

Mary found the white plastic shopping bag containing a framed color photograph in the trunk of his car. Bill removed the keys from his back pocket while walking across the teacher's parking lot. The silver frame held the snapshot of a teenage girl with curly blonde hair standing on the shore of a lake. He slid the key in the lock and turned it to the left. Judging by the faded colors and the girl's blouse, Mary decided that it had been taken in the mid-seventies. He closed the door and pulled the seatbelt across his chest. The girl was standing on the shore of what looked like Sylvian Beach with her jeans rolled up to her knees. He twisted the key in the ignition and placed his right foot on the gas. Small waves broke before her thin ankles and the broad expanse of blue sky behind her was cloudless. The digital clock on the dashboard indicated it was 4:05. Mary examined the girl's sensual pout. He drove the Jetta out of the parking lot. She slid the plastic bag over the picture, placed it where she had found it and quietly closed the trunk. He turned the headlights on before making a left onto Oneida Street. She stepped out of the garage and crossed the backyard as the first rays of the sun lightened the blue-gray sky. The heater blew warm stale air on Bill's face while the Jetta followed a line of cars up the street. She let herself in and placed his keys on the kitchen counter. The Jetta turned right onto Paris Hill Road and drove past a mechanized nativity scene. She crept upstairs and locked the bedroom door behind her. The late afternoon sky was streaked with long amber clouds. She retied the sash of her green robe and waited on the edge of the unmade bed. Bill thought about Sarah's gift in the trunk and wondered how she would react when given the photograph. A freight train slowly moved along the tracks a mile away from their house. The setting sun cast a bright orange glow across the horizon as he drove along Pinnacle Road. Twenty minutes later, she heard the door to his study open and close. He adjusted the heater as the car slowed with the traffic waiting to merge onto Route 8. She listened as the downstairs toilet flushed and waited patiently for him to leave before venturing downstairs. He glanced in the rearview mirror and yawned. A note on the kitchen table beneath his empty coffee cup stated that he would be home late and not to worry about dinner *I will fend for myself.* When an opening in the traffic appeared, he stepped on the gas and drove onto the long concrete ramp. The word love was scrawled above his name. The trees along the highway filtered the light from the setting sun. She crumpled up the note and threw it in the garbage can beneath the sink. He turned down the heater before activating the blinker. She sat in his chair and looked at the clock on the wall—the girl in the photograph looked vaguely familiar. Plastic wreaths hung from the streetlights and most of the storefronts were filled with Christmas decorations. A chickadee landed on the windowsill and pecked at the seeds in the bottom of the plastic feeder. He glanced at the clock on the dashboard and decided to take a shower before Sarah arrived. Sunlight filled the kitchen window as the realization struck her that the girl in the photograph was once one of his students and also his lover. He parked the car and took the key from the ignition. She held her head in her hands and began to cry. He retrieved the shopping bag from the trunk and walked across the parking lot.

Bill climbed the stairs and walked along the narrow concrete passageway overlooking the parking lot. Long lines of traffic moved along the four-lane road. He inserted the key in the lock, put his hand on the cold metal knob and turned it to the right. Two seventy-five watt bulbs inside the plastic chandelier hanging above the bed illuminated the room. He removed his jacket and draped it over the wooden chair near the door.

Sunday July 4, 1976

Sarah said, "God that was so embarrassing," before slamming the car door. Robert turned the key in the ignition, "What?" and placed his foot on the gas. "What?" she shook her head in exaggerated disbelief, "the way my mom was fawning all over you," the engine revved beneath the hood, "that's what." He placed his foot on the brake, "Well," and shifted the car into reverse, "at least she likes me." She winced, "I'm so sorry about that. I should have just waited for you outside," he shrugged as she continued, "that was just too weird," then turned to him, "why wasn't I adopted?" "You haven't met my mom yet," he placed his left hand on the steering wheel, "my mom is like," stretched his right arm across the top of the front seat, "the personification of weird," and looked over his shoulder. "Maybe we were both adopted then." He removed his foot from the brake, "If only that was the case," and the Falcon began moving backwards. "Well, I can *hardly wait* to meet her." "That's funny, Sarah," he turned the wheel to the left, "but I can't help but notice a hint of sarcasm in your voice right now," as the car turned onto the street. "How very perceptive of you." He pressed his foot on the brake and after the car came to a stop, he shifted into drive. They'd sat next to each other on the worn-out dark green couch in the living room. "Your mom likes her vodka though, huh?" He stepped on the gas and the car accelerated. He had tactfully answered a dozen of her mother's intoxicated questions while her father sat back in his recliner barely containing his contempt. "And your dad is a big guy," his right hand still ached a bit from their parting handshake, "I would not want to get on his bad side." She nodded, "No, you wouldn't." Her mother reminded her of the neighbor's barbecue *again* as they were trying to walk out the door. "So, do you think they liked me?" She shrugged, "I guess," and tried to obliterate the thought of spending the Fourth of July with her parents and the neighbors. "Seriously, do you think they do?" She imagined herself standing next to a pile of burning hamburgers while trading insults with people she hated. "Well, my mom does, that was pretty obvious. Don't you think?" He smiled, "Good." She leaned forward and turned the power knob on the car stereo, "I wished this worked." "I don't think it ever did," he pressed his foot on the brake, "Would you like me to sing you a song?" The car slowed before the intersection. "Something by Jim Nabors, perhaps?" She rested her right arm on the window frame and looked out at the curved telephone lines that ran for miles above their heads, "I think it's sweet that you care about that," beyond the swaying corn fields, the green pastures sparsely populated by black and white cows, the infrequent red barns and whitewashed farm houses. He looked from left to right. A broken yellow line divided the empty road in half. "About

94

what?" The road was bordered by broad bands of dust-colored gravel. He took his foot off the brake while slowly turning the steering wheel to the right. "About what my parents think of you." The car drove past a black and white sign indicating the posted speed. "I guess if they like me then maybe they'll trust me." "You know," she shook her head, "they don't really care all that much about what I do." A bank of white clouds moved away from the sun. "Really?" "Especially in summer," she turned to him, "as long as I don't get pregnant." He squinted through the glinting windshield, "Then why did your father look so angry?" "Because you were in his house and he had to acknowledge your presence." Robert was wearing a white T-shirt, "So, it had nothing to do with the fact that we're going out," faded blue jeans and a pair of blue Converse sneakers, "and that he doesn't approve." "Right," she nodded, "you could have been selling encyclopedias and he would have treated you the same way or worse," as her curly blonde hair was blown in the wind from the wide open car windows, "I told them I'm staying over at my brother's house tonight," she continued over the din, "I just need to call and tell him that's what I told them…just in case he calls the house." "There's a pay phone at the gas station," he looked down at the dashboard, "we need some gas anyway." A black Mustang swept past them in the incoming lane. "I don't have very much money." He grinned, "Ass or grass then," and noticed the sunlight on her bare thighs. "I knew you were going to say that." She looked out the window and watched the black telephone lines weave up and down between the weathered wooden poles before wondering out loud if the swallows perched on the lines could hear the conversations beneath them. He pointed at the glove compartment, "Open that." "Why?" "Just open it, you'll see." She opened the glove compartment and removed a clear plastic sandwich bag rolled into a thick oversized cigar shape. She looked at him, "Is this what I think it is?" then back at the bag. He nodded, "it's almost two grams," and stopped himself from telling her that he'd eaten a mouthful of them on the way over to her house, "It's going to make all of those fireworks, really work." She said, "I've only done mushrooms once before," and then recalled the time during Christmas vacation seven months ago when she and Laura had stayed up all night talking and laughing. He said, "They're a lot better than acid," while feeling the steering wheel vibrate in time with the rhythmic beats created by the creases in the road. Her eyes widened, "Oh," as she looked at him closely, "you've done that too?" "A lot better than acid," he nodded, "no comparison between the two of them," while clutching the steering wheel in his hands. "Are we going to do all of this ourselves?" "If you want," the tingling warmth in his chest was slowly spreading to the back of his head, "unless you think Laura and her boyfriend . . .what's his name again?" "Steve," she put the bag in the glove compartment, "he's pretty straight though," and closed the door, "I don't think that would be a very good idea." He saw the American flag grow larger in the distance long before he realized it was flying above the gas station. "We can do them all by ourselves if you want." She nodded, "I'd like that," with apprehension in her voice, "but not if we go to this party," and looked closely at his face, "that would just freak me out." Sarah was wearing a short pair of cut-off jeans, leather sandals, and a white dress shirt with the sleeves rolled up past her elbows and the top two buttons undone, "Is it okay that we don't go?" He took his foot off the gas, "We don't have to go," as the car began to slow down, "but I would like to trip with you," then pulled into the gas station and drove up to the pumps. She said, "So you can fuck with my head," as the car came to a stop. He nodded while fishing a dime out of his front pocket, "Exactly," and pressed it into her open palm. "Thank you, sweetie." She opened the car door as he turned off the engine and then he studied her long legs as they carried her toward the phone booth. The air was permeated by the smell of gas, and she felt the warmth of the sun on her shoulders. He wondered what it would be like to spend the rest of his life with her. The attendant emerged from the air-conditioned office and ogled her as he sauntered towards the Falcon. Maybe they could live together while she finished her last year of school? She heard the faint sound of a transistor radio tuned to a baseball game before the door closed. "Hey, buddy," the attendant's breath reeked of beer, "hey, buddy." She put her right hand on the door and pulled it open. Robert looked up at his pockmarked face and grease smeared brow, "Can I have five dollars worth of regular?" The booth reeked of urine and Coca-Cola. The attendant's narrow eyes were a watery gray and his thick black pompadour was slicked back into a tight duck's ass. She took the hot phone from its metal cradle and listened to the dial tone before dropping the dime in the slot. He heard the gas cap being unscrewed, and then the pump's nozzle was inserted into the car. She dialed the number and stepped as far away from the booth as the metal cord attached to the receiver would allow. He leaned forward and examined the pulverized remains of a large gray moth that had slammed into the center of the windshield. She could her the phone ringing while she held the receiver a few inches away from her ear. He heard the pump activate as he leaned back in his seat and gas began pouring into the tank. She thought of the phone lines they had driven below as it rang again. The attendant reappeared in front of the car and began smearing a squeegee across the windshield. She thought of the beige telephone mounted on her brother's kitchen wall as it rang again. The tingling warmth in his chest spread through his arms as he sank deeper into the seat. She imagined her brother putting down a novel, getting up from the lawn chair, and walking to the screen door as the phone rang again. Thin trails of gray water ran down the windshield as the moth disappeared beneath the rubber sponge. She cleared her throat in anticipation as the phone rang again. He watched the droplets of water that hung on the window reflect tiny prisms of rainbow colored light that made him think of diamonds as they slowly evaporated in the heat of the afternoon sun. The phone rang again, and she began to wonder where her brother could be. The bell on the pump dinged and Robert looked over at Sarah, who was standing outside the phone booth holding the receiver a few inches away from her left ear. She made eye contact with Robert as the phone rang again. The attendant was positioned above the window, "Hey, buddy," and holding out his greasy right hand. She hoped he was out working in the garage and that was why he wasn't answering. He leaned forward and removed the wallet from the back pocket of his jeans. She sighed as the phone rang again and decided to let it ring two more times before hanging up. He extracted a five and noticed the large green prison tattoo of a swastika on the attendant's right forearm. The phone rang again as she watched the distant heat vapors rising above the road. As the attendant's fist closed around the bill, Robert reached the immediate conclusion that he'd probably done the tattoo himself, while serving a fifteen-year stretch for raping a teenage hitchhiker. She hung up and pulled the door closed before walking toward the car. He turned the key in the ignition and placed his foot on the gas. She heard the revving engine and quickened her pace. The attendant watched her sit down, "have a happy Fourth of July," and swing her legs into the car. She looked up at him with a forced smile and slammed the door. Robert shifted into drive and pulled the car back onto the road. "What was that all about?" He stepped on the gas, "He had this huge swastika on his arm," and looked at her, "I think he's a Nazi or a child molester or something." "Probably both," she offered before asking, "Where do they find those people?" "Attica," he flatly suggested. She looked out the window as they passed a dilapidated barn with a collapsed roof and frowned. "You look upset, what did he say?" A line of four cars drove past them in the incoming lane. "He didn't answer." "Maybe he went to that party." She shook her head, "You don't know my brother." "Oh, yeah?" "That is the last thing he would be doing today." He looked in the rearview mirror. "Could we just drive over there and say hello?" The road behind them was empty. "I haven't seen him in awhile." "Where does he live?" "Down near Clayville, it's not very far from here." "You're worried about him, aren't you?" She nodded, "Kinda," and watched the expression on his face, "this isn't exactly his favorite holiday." He shrugged, "If that's what you want to do," and looked in the rearview mirror again. "Are you sure you don't mind if we don't go to that party?" "It's fine with me." She said, "It's not that I don't want to be seen with you, it's just that," then let her words drift out the open window. He took his foot off the gas, "I really don't care what we do," and the car slowed down. "That's what I like about you." He placed his foot on the brake, "What's that?" "You are so easy to please." He smiled while rolling the steering wheel to the left, "Not really," as the car made a U-turn. "Oh no?" And then accelerated. He looked into her eyes, "It's enough just to spend time with you," as she smiled, "it doesn't really matter what we do." She slid across the dark blue vinyl seat and kissed him on the cheek. He wanted to say that he had already fallen in love with her. She put her left arm around his shoulders and kissed him on the corner of his mouth. She was so unlike any girl he had ever gone out with, and he couldn't believe his luck. He wanted to take her away from that awful house and save her from her parents. A state trooper swept past them in the incoming lane. He watched the car speed away in the rearview mirror, "Do you think that's why your mom drinks?" She had her right hand on his thigh, "What do you mean?" "Because your brother got…got hurt in Vietnam?" She shook her head, "No." "I just thought that maybe—" "My mom drinks like that," clearing her throat, "because she married a man who beats the shit out of her all the time." Her response weighed on his chest, "He seems like the type." "You know," she looked out the window as they drove past the gas station, "I forgot your dime." "It's the creep's tip, then." She nodded, "It's not as bad as it was before," and turned to him, "now that he's working again he isn't home all that much." They drove past a opossum that hadn't made it across the road. "Why do you think she stays with him?" The smell of its corpse lingered in the car. "She doesn't know any better." "It's that simple?" He sounded incredulous. She nodded, "Well, it is." He gripped the steering wheel, "Does he ever hit you?" Two hawks were circling a hundred yards above the road they were driving along. "So when did you do LSD?" He removed his foot from the gas, "Last spring at this big college party in Utica," and touched the brake with the tip of his sneaker. The car slowed before the stop sign. "With that girl?" He looked from left to right, "And her roommate." A broken yellow line divided the empty road in half. "And her roommate?" The Queen Anne's lace growing alongside the road swayed in a warm breeze. "It was kind of weird though," he took his foot off the brake, "I shouldn't be telling you this." "Now you'll have to." The Falcon turned right and drove past a black and white sign indicating the posted speed. "But you didn't answer my question." She ignored him, "Did you have sex with *both* of them?" "Sorta," he began to blush, "I mean to the extent that we could." She pinched him on the arm, "What does that mean?" "Ouch," he looked at her, "that hurt." "Sorry," she playfully caressed the spot she pinched the way a child is taught to pet a kitten, and in a soft voice repeated her question. "It was more mental than physical." The car sped past a row of trees before descending a hill. "What does that mean?" "The feeling of desire was more fulfilling." "So, did you have sex with them?" "Just oral sex." With a smirk, "You mean you went down on both of them?" He had spent the night tripping in a double bed with two college sophomores, "Yeah." They had treated him more like a pet or a stuffed animal. "And did they reciprocate?" He sighed, "Sorta." She began to laugh, "They didn't, did they?" "But that wasn't the point." The car sped past a large red barn with a black roof. "It really wasn't about sex as much as it was about desire." She looked out the window and pointed, "Make a left here." He removed his foot from the gas and activated the blinker, "I mean," the car slowed before the turn, "don't you think you can love more than one person at a time?" "I guess so," she realized she hadn't thought about Bill all afternoon, "why do you ask?" He looked out at a field of swaying grass while thinking of an answer. She said, "It's right here," before he had a chance to explain, "on the left." The car slowed as it approached the house. "Oh, well I guess he's fine." A battered Volkswagen bus coated in primer and a black Harley Davidson chopper were parked in the middle of the overgrown lawn. "Do you think we should stop and say hello?" "No," she shook her head, "not when he's with his crazy friends," and pressed her hand on his thigh, "I'll introduce you to him some other time." The car pulled away. "I know a place we can go." He scratched his chin, "Oh yeah?" "We can go swimming if you want." "I didn't bring my trunks." "That's okay, neither did I." "Oh," he turned to her, "well in that case," with a broad grin. She opened the glove compartment, "So, what were you saying before," and removed the bag of mushrooms, "about loving more than one person at a time?" He watched her unroll the bag, "I don't mean for a lifetime but in a moment or for a night." She sniffed the contents before saying, "You sound like such a hippie sometimes." He turned the steering wheel to the left, "Don't call me names," as the car climbed a small hill, "just answer the question," and the road narrowed. Tall trees hung over the road and blocked out the sky. She removed a mushroom from the bag, "Okay, I will," placed it in her mouth and began to chew.

Donald Breckenridge is the author of more than a dozen plays as well as the novella *Rockaway Wherein* (Red Dust, 1998) and the novels *6/2/95* (Spuyten Duyvil, 2002) and *You Are Here* (Starcherone Books, 2009). In addition, he is the fiction editor of *The Brooklyn Rail*, co-editor of the *InTranslation* website and editor of *The Brooklyn Rail Fiction Anthology* (Hanging Loose Press, 2006). He is working on his fourth novel.